Yellow Ribbons

Other Avalon Books by Jane Edwards

DANGEROUS ODYSSEY
TERROR BY DESIGN
THE HESITANT HEART
THE GHOST OF CASTLE KILGARROM
SUSANNAH IS MISSING!

Yellow Ribbons

JANE EDWARDS

AVALON BOOKS
THOMAS BOUREGY AND COMPANY, INC.
401 LAFAYETTE STREET
NEW YORK, NEW YORK 10003

Library of Congress Catalog Card Number: 91-92219
ISBN 0-8034-8892-0

PRINTED IN THE UNITED STATES OF AMERICA
ON ACID-FREE PAPER
BY HADDON CRAFTSMEN, SCRANTON, PENNSYLVANIA

This book is for

All the troops who were sent to serve in the Persian Gulf
during our recent war with Iraq;

and

All of us at home, who wrote the letters
and tied the yellow ribbons
for their safe return;

and
most especially for

Valued friends and neighbors John (U.S.M.C., Retired)
and Jayne Christjansen, who patiently answered
a million questions about The Corps.

Thank you!

Chapter One

September 10, 1990

Any Marine
Operation Desert Shield
FPO NY NY 09866–0006

Dear Marine:

Hello! We hope you are feeling good. Are you staying safe there in the desert and not being too lonesome? It must be a weird place, with sand everywhere and no trees or mountains. Here in Spruce Ridge, Oregon, it is just the opposite.

Our teacher, Ms. Smith, says it gets real hot where you are. Did you bring your swimsuit in case you find an oasis where you can cool off? There is a picture of an oasis in our geography book. It shows people riding on camels. Some palm trees are growing near there. If you see one of those, look up. You might find some dates, and they are good to eat.

There are fourteen of us students in the fifth grade here at Timberline School. All of us would like to write to everyone who was sent far away to protect freedom. Since we can't, our class took a vote. We picked the Marine Corps for our special heroes. So you are the one to get this letter, not somebody in the Navy or Army or Air Force. They are doing a good job too, of course.

Here are a few things to make you laugh and forget there might be a war. Some are cartoons. Some are comic strips, like Doonesbury. Pretty funny, huh?

If you will answer our letter, we promise to write back.

Your friends,
April, Beth, Carlos, Frank, Greg, Ingrid, Jamie, Katy, Kevin, Megan, Moose, Penny, Ted, and Zach

P.S. Ms. Smith says next time we'll go backward in the alphabet. That way Zach can sign his name first.

October 2, 1990

Ms. Smith's Fifth Grade Class
Timberline School
Sawmill Road
Spruce Ridge, Oregon, U.S.A.

Dear April, Beth, Carlos, Frank, Greg, Ingrid, Jamie, Katy, Kevin, Megan, Moose, Penny, Ted, and Zach,

Your letter came today. It sure was welcome. Last night we had a big sandstorm. It blew grit into everything, even the toothpaste. Hearing from fourteen new friends and laughing at the cartoons you sent made me feel much better.

Spruce Ridge sounds like the little town in Washington State where I grew up. We had a sawmill there, plus plenty of trees and a lot of rain. They could use more of both those things in Saudi Arabia. Ms. Smith is right about it being hot here. I haven't found an oasis yet. If I do, I'll be sure to keep an eye out for the dates. They would make a nice change from the MREs we get out on maneuvers. That means Meals Ready to Eat.

We keep busy training and learning how to get along in the desert. The Bedouins have shown us a few tricks to avoid danger. They are experts at survival. The camel riders you see in your geography book are probably from a tribe of these nomads. These days they have a new way of getting around. When the Saudi government got rich from selling oil, they bought a pickup truck for every Bedouin family. Here is a snap-

shot I took of one of those trucks, with a camel tethered to the back of it. I have a hunch the desert people don't place much faith in machinery.

Yes, I'm feeling good. The Marine Corps is my home, so I'm not really lonesome. Being halfway around the world is much harder on some of my men who have families back in the States. But everyone's morale is high.

Thanks again for your letter, kids. Keep them coming. It takes the mail a few weeks to travel the 11,000 miles between there and here. Don't worry if you don't hear back from me right away. I will always answer if I possibly can.

Your buddy,
Alexander Ross MacKinnon
Captain, USMC

P.S. My friends call me Mack.

October 19, 1990

Dear Mack,

Wow, you really did answer us! So did two other marines. One is a lance corporal called Austin. Owen is our other new friend. He drives a tank. It's great to have all three of you for pen pals.

That was a neat picture you sent of the camel hitched up to the pickup truck. It is tacked to our bulletin board for everyone to look at. Your letter too. Yea to the Bedouin people for helping you. Our class has started a special project to learn more about them. We want to find out what they eat besides dates. Also, how come they wander around and camp out in tents instead of living in a regular town.

Pretty soon it will be Halloween. Do you know if the kids there in Saudi Arabia go trick-or-treating? Ms. Smith says she doubts it. That is because their customs are much different from ours. But just in case, we are mailing you a bag of candy corn. Also some peanuts. They won't melt, even when they get real hot. You can give part of them to the trick-or-treaters if they do come around. The rest are for you to eat. We stuck in our favorite kind of toothpaste too. It's sealed up tight in a plastic bag to keep the sand out.

Love from your friends,
Zach, Ted, Penny, Moose, Megan, Kevin, Katy, Jamie, Ingrid, Greg, Frank, Carlos, Beth, and April

October 20, 1990

Dear Mack,

I hope you don't mind if I write you special. Just by myself, I mean. Ms. Smith said she was sure it would be okay. She copyed down your address for me to take home. But I know Captains are very busy people. So I will understand if you don't get around to answering me as quick as when the whole class writes you all together.

Is the Marine Corps really your home? I thought it

was your job. One nice thing, you always have plenty of guys to talk to. I wish I did. Granny Sophie doesn't say much anymore. Sometimes she doesn't even remember who I am. That is a secret between you and me, Mack. I wouldn't want the other kids to know about it. They might think she was not right in the head. I figure it's probly just flu, don't you think?

I wish you could come to our class Halloween party. Maybe at Christmas the general will give you a vacation. Could you visit us then?

Your good friend,
Jamie Dawson

November 7, 1990

Dear Zach, Ted, Penny, Moose, Megan, Kevin, Katy, Jamie, Ingrid, Greg, Frank, Carlos, Beth, and April,

Happy Halloween a little late. The Company just got back from an eight-day field operation. Our three rifle platoons and the weapons platoon teamed up with a group of French artillery units. Some American M-60 tanks were out on maneuvers at the same time. I thought about your friend Owen when I saw them. Maybe he was one of the drivers helping to level off berms. Those are the high ridges of sand dunes we have to cross on foot.

Thank you for the peanuts and candy corn. It's been more than twenty years since I tasted candy corn. Not since I was about ten or so. I guess that's about your age, isn't it? Also, it was good to get the toothpaste.

The cutouts you sent of the black cats and pumpkins kept us reminded of the holidays coming up back home.

Your teacher guessed right. Nobody goes trick-or-treating in Saudi. Town kids seem to have fun playing soccer in the streets, though. Just the boys, of course. The girls don't get out much. We never see them at all, except in the bazaars. Then they wear veils over their hair and across their faces.

Take care.

Your buddy,
Mack

November 10, 1990

Dear Jamie,

It was a nice surprise to get the special letter you wrote me. Don't worry, I can always make time to drop a line to friends, whether it's one or fourteen. But I'm a long way off, remember. If anything is bothering you, it would be a good idea to talk it over with an adult who can give you on-the-spot advice.

Hope Granny Sophie is feeling better. Flu can be nasty stuff. Did she go to the doctor for a checkup? She isn't the only person you have for company, is she? How about your parents? Got any brothers and sisters?

Sure, being a marine is my job. But the Corps is also my home, because I live on base even back in the States. I'm in charge of a whole company, 230 men. But that doesn't always mean I have a lot of close friends. I have to give them orders, and they have to trust me not to get them killed. It's kind of a tricky situation.

The evenings are starting to get cooler now. Sometimes, after duty hours, we fly kites and see how far up we can get them. I never did that when I was growing up. Back then, there were always too many trees around for the kite strings to get tangled in. But here in Saudi that isn't one of our problems.

You have a good Thanksgiving, Jamie. Keep in touch.

Your friend,
Mack

November 26, 1990

Dear Mack,

Merry Christmas! We are sending you this package real early. That way you will be sure to get it in time. All of us found things to put in that we hoped you would like. Such as books and games, sunburn lotion and paper to write on, chewing gum and a yo-yo.

Also, last Saturday we went to Ms. Smith's house to make cookies. We are sending you the ones that didn't burn. Everybody got to decorate one for you any way they wanted. We are sending some to Austin and Owen too.

Love from your friends,
April, Beth, Carlos, Frank, Greg, Ingrid, Jamie, Katy, Kevin, Megan, Moose, Penny, Ted, and Zach

November 26, 1990

Dear Mack,

Today in class we packed a box of presents to send you. Do you like sugar cookies? Mine is decorated with a star in green frosting. A long time ago the Wise Men followed a star through the desert. So that is why I drew it, because you are in the desert.

I changed my mind about Granny Sophie having flu. She doesn't cough or throw up like I did when I had it. Mostly she just sits in her rocking chair and looks out the window. It doesn't bother me much when she calls me Warren. He was my grandfather. I guess she must be thinking of the good old days.

Me too. The best old days was when me and my Mom lived at the beach for a whole summer. Here is a picture of a wild flower she painted there. Ms. Smith says being a Marine is a very important job, and you can't come visit until it's all finished. So I am sending this to say Merry Christmas from me.

Your real true friend,
Jamie D.

December 1, 1990

Dear April, Beth, Carlos, Frank, Greg, Ingrid, Jamie, Katy, Kevin, Megan, Moose, Penny, Ted, and Zach,

The mail has been moving pretty well. With luck, you will get this package before school lets out for the holidays. I had a chance to go into Riyadh the other day. It's Saudi's big city, and the bazaars there are fun places to shop. The perfect spot to buy a few souvenirs for friends.

The dark head scarf is called a burnoose. Men and boys wear them in the desert to keep the sun off their heads. Here, once a girl gets to be ten years old, she stops playing with her brothers and moves to the women's part of her house full-time. This is the kind of nose veil she wears across her face when visitors come around. Aren't you girls glad you live in Oregon instead of over here?

The Arabs love chocolate. Here's a local candy bar for each of you. Fifteen in all. That includes one for Ms. Smith. I'm also tucking in a few pieces of Saudi money I got in change. They are called dinars and riyals. The newspaper is the Arab News. *That's what they tell me, anyway. To me, the writing looks almost slippery, the way it slides across the page. It's hard to tell where one word ends and the next one starts up. Thought you might have fun sampling our field rations too, the MREs. Not the tastiest stuff in the world, but they keep us going.*

The last thing is a banner I made to put up in your classroom if you want. Though it says "One Million Thanks To The Gang," that's an understatement. You deserve ten times that many hugs and pats on the back for all the letters and good cheer you've sent my way.

Happy holidays to every one of you!

Mack

December 28, 1990

Dear Ms. Smith:

The wonderful box of Christmas gifts just arrived. I've already dropped the class a note on one of the new sheets of writing paper to thank them. But I have a hunch a lot of the credit is due to you. The kind of effort that went into those cookies was above and beyond the call of duty, as we say in the Corps. You must be a terrific sport, letting them use your place for the project. Got it cleaned up yet? Take my word, every crumb was appreciated.

I need to discuss another topic with you that isn't so cheery. For all I know, there may be no cause for alarm, but the possibility has been keeping me awake nights. You are the only adult I know of in Spruce Ridge, Ms. Smith, so I'm going to ask you to give me a hand finding out what's what.

I have received several letters from Jamie Dawson, one of your students. He sounds like a great little kid. And a worried one. Just reading between the lines, I get the impression this youngster is struggling with a predicament he isn't old enough to handle.

It sounds to me as if the boy lives with a senile grandmother. What about the rest of his family? Though he sent me a beautiful little watercolor his mother painted, he evades my questions about his parents. The only relative he mentions is Granny Sophie. The fact that she does not recognize him—even calls him by the wrong name—is causing Jamie deep concern.

I'm flattered to have been trusted with this child's secrets. The problem is, I'm too far away to do anything but listen.

What we need here is some strategic reconnaissance. Could you see what you can find out? Discreetly? Jamie particularly requested that I not mention Granny Sophie's illness to his classmates. I know he would be hurt if he thought I stuck my nose in where it doesn't belong and blew the whistle on him. So this is strictly between you and me. If Jamie's folks are handling the situation, I'll gladly butt out and mind my own business.

Tension is mounting here in Saudi as the deadline for war approaches. Most of us believe that combat is inevitable. My major concern must be the safety of my men as we prepare to go into battle. They are counting on me for leadership. I don't intend to let them down. You can take one extra worry off my shoulders by letting me know that Jamie is all right. If money is a problem for him, I'll be happy to pitch in.

My best wishes to you and the class for the New Year.

Yours,

A. R. MacKinnon

January 15, 1991

Dear Captain MacKinnon:

By now you should have received letters from the class thanking you for the gifts. Everyone in town has been in to admire them. Our schoolroom has become a small museum of Arabian curios. We are all very grateful for your generosity in sharing your Middle East experience with us.

I am sorry to report that your fears about Jamie Dawson were correct. Here in Spruce Ridge, the people are friendly, but as in small communities everywhere, they are also reticent about their private affairs. Since arriving in September, I've tried hard to give the children a good education without meddling in anyone's personal life. But even neighbors who have known Jamie for years were astonished to learn of the problems he was trying to cope with alone.

As soon as your letter arrived, I enlisted the help of the town doctor, who filled me in on Jamie's background. Granny Sophie, who is eighty-three, is his great-grandmother. He and his mother came to live with Granny after his father was killed in a logging accident a few years ago. I gather that Jessie Dawson used to support them all with her paintings until her death about a year ago, when her car stalled on a mountain road during a blizzard.

Dr. Taherne assures me that until quite recently Granny was a competent guardian for the boy. When Alzheimer's disease began affecting her last fall, Jamie took on all the household chores himself. He kept hoping that if he took good care of Granny, she would recover rather than die, as his parents had done. Jamie's worst fear is that he might have to leave Spruce Ridge and live in a foster home.

The families of my other students are making sure that won't happen, at least not until the end of the school year. Granny Sophie has been taken to a nursing home in Salem, where she will receive good care. Jamie is being welcomed into his classmates' homes. Each family will take a turn at making room for him. Moving around every week is hardly an ideal solution, and of course some permanent arrangement will need to be made this summer. But right now Jamie needs to be with people he knows and trusts.

I have told Dr. Taherne about your kind offer of financial help. If money becomes a problem, we will be sure to let you know.

Thank you, Captain MacKinnon, for recognizing Jamie's dilemma and calling our attention to it. He's going to be fine now. I wish it were possible to wire or telephone you to set your mind at ease about him immediately. With the President's deadline about to expire, you have many urgent concerns right there in the Gulf.

God keep you all safe.

H. A. Smith, Fifth-Grade Teacher
Timberline School

January 17, 1991

Operation DESERT STORM

Dear Mack,

Ms. Smith says she told you about Granny Sophie going to the hospital. At first I was real mad at her and the doctor. I told them to go away. I said we didn't need them around. But I guess that wasn't true. It's probly a good thing Granny doesn't have to count on me to buy grocerys and haul in the wood and bring the wash to town on my bike any more. Right now the snowdrifts are up to my chin.

I am living with the other kids in my class. This week at Kevin's house. His Mom made us pancakes for breakfast. They were great.

The TV says the war has started up for real now. It is called OPERATION DESERT STORM. They showed pictures of lots of marines getting ready for battle. Was one of them you? I think maybe so. They were in the desert too.

Here is a piece of yellow ribbon. We put a big long one up all around our classroom. And a bow on the door. There is more tied on the school fence too. The yellow ribbons mean we want all our troops to come home safe.

Mack, I got it figured out that you told Ms. Smith about Granny. I think you did it because you worried about me like I am doing about you now. So I forgive you. It's all right. I am still your friend.

Jamie D.

January 31, 1991

Dear Jamie,

Hearing that you are still my friend took a big load off my mind. It's true, son. I did write Ms. Smith to say I was worried about you and Granny. I couldn't be there to do it myself, so I asked her to check and make sure you were okay. I knew she would do her best for you.

Teamwork is real important when you're in the Marines. The other men and I are all part of platoons and companies. That way we can count on each other when the going gets tough. I thought you needed someone to depend on who was right there in Spruce Ridge. If you have any more problems, write and tell me about them. I'll try my best to help you handle them. But tell Ms. Smith too, will you, buddy?

Thank you for the yellow ribbon. I keep it in my pocket where I can take it out and look at it every so often. It reminds me of all the good friends like you I have back home. I'm looking forward to heading for Oregon and meeting you someday when we've finished what we came over here to do.

Even though I thanked you for it before, I want to tell you again how much I like the beautiful picture of the wildflower your mother painted. I keep it up where all the men and I can see it.

Love,
Mack

February 1, 1991

Dear Mack,

This big red heart says Happy Valentine's Day to you from the whole class. Plus, we are each sending little cards to you with special valentines on them. And heart candy too.

YOU ARE OUR VALENTINE!!!!!

Those SCUD missiles sound really awful. If you hear one go over, keep your head down and your helmet buckled tight. The poor camels must be scared too with all the noise in their desert.

Hearts from,
April, Beth, Carlos, Frank, Greg, Ingrid, Jamie, Katy, Kevin, Megan, Moose, Penny, Ted, and Zach

February 17, 1991

Dear Mack,

The TV here at Penny's house says the ground war has started up now. That means your company is going to fight, I bet. Those MREs you put in with our Christmas presents didn't taste real great. The eggs, especialy. But I know your cook won't have time to make hamburgers and gravy and pie for everyone if you are marching through the sand. So it's good you have the MREs and won't go hungry.

I am glad you liked the picture. There are a couple more packed away with the stuff Ms. Smith is keeping for me. Most of them got sold, though. The lady at the craft store always wanted a whole bunch. I heard her tell my Mom once that the tourists who came to the beach on vacation bought them quicker than she could hang them up.

On Friday my teacher called up to see how Granny Sophie was feeling. We keep hoping she will get better and remember me, so I can go visit her. Ms. Smith said she would drive me to Salem if the doctors said it was okay for me to come. But they didn't.

I am trying not to worry like you said, but it is hard. Next week I will be living at Ted's house. He has a horse named Bucko. While I am there I will take a look around the barn to see if I can find one of Bucko's old shoes to send you. That is because horseshoes are for good luck.

You never said Love Mack in your letters before. Was that just to make me feel good? Even if it was, I love you too.

Your real true loving friend,
Jamie D.

February 28, 1991

Dear Mack,

ALL RIGHT! CEASE FIRE! Yea for the Marines! And the other troops too, of course. Ms. Smith says we won't take the yellow ribbons down until you come home. So they are still up all over the place. . . .

Love,

Zach, Ted, Penny, Moose, Megan, Kevin, Katy, Jamie, Ingrid, Greg, Frank, Carlos, Beth, and April

March 11, 1991

Dear Captain MacKinnon:

I thought it was wisest to share our sad news with you. If you should catch an extra note of anxiety in the children's next few letters, it is because we just learned that one of the class's other pen pals was killed in action during Desert Storm. Austin Yakich was a young lance corporal from Pennsylvania. His parents wrote to tell us of their loss after finding our Christmas cards among his effects.

You will be happy to know that Jamie is doing pretty well. He calls himself a Bedouin, making a joke out of the fact that he moves around from place to place every week, rather like the nomads do. He's a booster of those tribesmen because you once said they helped the Marine Corps.

I'm sure there is no need to tell you that you have become a shining role model for this youngster. It's hopeless to think that he will ever be reunited with Granny Sophie. The nursing home doctor tells me she is slipping away rapidly and has only a few weeks left to live. But knowing you are out there at the end of an FPO number gives a tremendous boost to Jamie's morale.

Many, many thanks for your letters to him, and to the class as a group. It's above and beyond, as you would say, for you to keep on writing with so many other heavy demands on your time. Naturally, mail call is everyone's favorite period of the day. I'd say it outranks arithmetic about a thousand to one!

Sincerely yours,
H. A. Smith

March 25, 1991

Dear Zach, Ted, Penny, Moose, Megan, Kevin, Katy, Jamie, Ingrid, Greg, Frank, Carlos, Beth, and April,

Thanks for the fantastic valentines! Believe it or not, they just arrived. Lately our mail has been very slow in catching up to us. Our company has been given a special assignment, and we have been moving from spot to spot. A lot of American troops are on their way home already. What we are doing is tracking down MIAs to make sure everyone gets back. And we have had good luck finding servicemen listed as missing in action. Found a half dozen men three days ago. They were being held prisoner by Iraqi soldiers who didn't even know the war was over!

Sorry this is so short. Got a meeting with the brass in five minutes. We will be heading back down to Kuwait when our mission is complete. When we arrive, I'll see what the bazaars there have in the way of souvenirs for you.

Your buddy,
Mack

March 25, 1991

Dear Jamie,

Your valentine was one of the best. It's a real pleasure to see your name in the corner of an envelope at mail call. Your letters always make me feel good. Keep them coming if you have time.

Like I told the class in my other letter, the company has been out on special assignment. Doing a little rescue work. I'd like to be on my way home right now, but this is important.

I'm sorry to hear you haven't been able to visit Granny Sophie. When you're sick, it's important to get all the rest you can, you know. But it was good of Ms. Smith to offer to drive you all the way to Salem.

I still have my wildflower picture safe. I enjoy looking at it, especially since the only other thing around here I can see is scorching sand. And a few other grubby marines, of course.

You bet I meant it when I signed my letter with love. That isn't a word I've had a chance to use much in the past. But coming from me to you, it's straight from my heart.

Love,
Mack

April 22, 1991

Dear Mack,

Ms. Smith said she told you about Austin getting killed. We sure felt bad. Would you think I was a wimp if I said I cried? Well, I did.

Are you still out in the desert, hunting for the Missing in Action people? We got your letters a while back. We have been wondering where you are now.

The snow is gone. Flowers are blooming all over the place. Out in the woods the other day I saw some violets. Those were my Mom's favrites. She used to joke that her name ought to be Violet or Lily instead of just plain Jessie.

When are you coming home, Mack? The yellow ribbon is starting to get kind of dusty.

Whole big Oregon sand hills of love,
Jamie

May 2, 1991

Dear Mack,

School ends next month. After that I won't be living in Spruce Ridge any more. The other day, a man and lady came to talk to me at Frank's house. They said it was their job to find me a place in a foster home. I asked could they find it here in town. They said no. This town was too small. So I will have to go live in a city. But I don't want to. What if the post office can't find me to deliver your letters when you write again?

I never could find that horseshoe of Bucko's. That worried me. I got a hunch you really need good luck. So today I went out after school and looked everywhere until I found a four leaf clover. Here it is. That is better luck even than horseshoes. I sure hope it works.

I love you,
Jamie

May 11, 1991

Dear Mack,

Here at Moose's house there is a big book of maps called a road atlas. I looked in there to see if anyplace else besides Oregon has a Spruce Ridge. No. There is a Spruce Pine in North Carolina, where Ms. Smith used to live. Outside of that, no Spruces at all. So I guess your letters didn't go to the wrong state.

I have been wondering if one of those SCUD missiles got loose and bombed your post office. Did that happen? If so, that must be where your letters are. Blowed up. Otherwise, I don't know what could have happened to them.

Here is another piece of yellow ribbon. I found it in the street and rubbed the dirt off with a wet rag. That is how come it is wrinkled. But it still means the same thing as always.

Mack, I know you said not to worry. But I can't help it. If you can't come home, could you just write two words on a card? Please say I'M OKAY. All of us would be real happy to hear that. Me especialy.

Love,

Jamie

May 16, 1991

Dear Mack,

My Granny Sophie is dead. Just like my father and mother and Austin. I am figuring out that I must be bad luck. Because every one I really and truly love dies. So I think it would be better not to love you any more. That way maybe you will be safe after all.

This week I am staying with my teacher. I get to sleep in a rollaway bed up in her loft. We borrowed it from Beth's aunt. The rollaway bed, I mean, not the loft. Last night Ms. Smith made me cocoa with marsh-melows in it. She said it would give me sweet dreams. But it didn't. I couldn't stop thinking about that foster home. What if the other kids there are mean? What if they have a dog who bites?

I could manage those things okay if I knew you would write me there. But I am starting to give up hope about that. I have been working out what a Bedouin would do, and I know what kind of place they would go to.

For now I am still here, tho, Mack. I go to the post

office every day. Sometimes twice. Please write and say you are not killed in action like Austin.

Your friend,
Jamie D.

May 27, 1991

Dear Mack,

This morning when we came in our classroom, a strange lady was there. She said Hello. I am Ms. Crandall, your substitute teacher. Our real teacher had to leave all of a sudden, she said.

I sure can't figure Ms. Smith not even waiting to tell us goodbye. Katy's mother said a mergency must have happened over the weekend. She told me don't worry. Ms. Smith is fine, she said, and will be back soon. But Mack, everyone thought you would come right home after the war, and you never did.

It must be my fault. Jamie D. the jinx. It was too hard not to love Ms. Smith. Now if she has bad luck and doesn't come back just like you, I am to blame for sure.

Mack, I am real tired of worrying about people I love. like. I am borrowing this stamp from Katy's father to say so long. When I leave maybe good luck will start happening again. For you and Ms. Smith and everyone. Some other kid can take my spot in the foster home. I am going to find the good old days.

Goodbye,
Jamie D.

Chapter Two

Day in and day out, logging trucks rumbled past the cabin, tackling the arduous climb between the Rainbow Springs Sawmill and the summit of Brother-in-Law Mountain. Always, after straining up the Timberline grade, they would shift down at the plateau a hundred yards farther up the road, mustering power for the next part of the steep ascent.

If Holly happened to be outside, planting bulbs or washing her van as she was today, she'd spot them wheezing back down again, hours later. They were now loaded with the gigantic logs that were the lifeblood of Spruce Ridge and hundreds of similar small communities all over the Northwest.

Some of the trees were as thick around as she was tall. Last summer she'd almost wept to see them toppled and then hauled ignominiously off to be planed into board feet of lumber from which homes and stores and barns could be constructed. Holly soon learned, however, that timber firms planted five new trees for every one felled by the lumberjacks, that without the logging industry, nine out of ten families in this part of Oregon would be out of work and living on public welfare.

Empty or loaded, the rigs were such a commonplace sight that she seldom bothered to glance up when one of them passed. But this Saturday in mid-June, one nudged her attention by pausing at the plateau, just long enough to drop somebody off on the side of the road.

''Thanks for the lift, buddy,'' a man's voice floated downhill to her on the crisp, clear air.

''Anytime.''

The trucker's response was muffled by the clash of shifting gears. The engine roared as the behemoth tractor-trailer continued on up the grade.

Overhead, the sun was a dazzling ball of flame in the smogless sky. Holly crimped the hose, stemming the gush of water, and then shaded her eyes. To spare the lenses a splattering with grimy soapsuds, she usually groped her way through this particular job without her eyeglasses. Now she was sorry she'd left them inside. Even streaked, they would have given her a better view of the tall, lean figure picking his way toward her along the road.

By squinting, she managed to make out a few details.

His right arm was braced across his chest, held in a dark sling. From his left hand dangled a small flight bag. Faded denims clung to his long legs. A matching jacket was draped across his shoulders. He had the deepest tan she'd ever seen, and the shortest haircut.

Holly caught her breath, and then forced it out again. She had to quit doing that! Time and again in the past few months she'd caught herself staring anxiously at unfamiliar men, wondering and wishing. Such undignified behavior had netted her three spontaneous proposals of marriage, along with fourteen somewhat less flattering propositions. Not to mention numerous indignant comments from female companions of the men doing the proposing or propositioning.

It was no use, she told herself for the hundredth time. He wasn't coming back. Something terrible had happened to him. It must have. Otherwise, he never would have let the children down. It was tearing her apart to go on hoping and praying and keeping that bedraggled yellow ribbon looped around the maple tree in the middle of the lawn.

Uneasily, Holly watched the stranger approach. Why would a hitchhiker ask to be dropped off in this isolated spot? A family named Allardyce lived up around the next curve, but he was heading in the wrong direction to visit them. Below the small A-frame where she lived, houses on the grade were few and far between.

This must be his destination. But no one she knew went around bumming rides from truckers.

Instinctively, she tightened her grip on the hose. At

five feet two and weighing a scant hundred pounds, she'd be no physical match for a man, even for one with an arm in a sling. But she'd taken a few self-defense courses and learned a few tricks. A blast of cold water in the face would discourage any predator, man or beast.

He slowed as he reached the gate of her winding front path. "Looking for someone?" Holly called.

Surprised, he turned his head and caught sight of her standing there.

"Yes," he answered, not trespassing, but just staying where he was. "A lady named Smith, a schoolteacher. I'm told that this is where she lives. Is that your mom?"

It was a reasonable question, Holly supposed, trying to stifle her quick resentment. Barefoot, with her silky blond hair skinned back into a long pigtail dangling down her back, she probably did look like a teenager. Especially in the ancient T-shirt and fraying shorts she'd put on to cope with this grubby job.

She shook her head, wishing again for the big, round eyeglasses that made the world and everything in it a whole lot more visible.

"No," she answered flatly. "Who's asking?"

"My name is MacKinnon."

The hose spurted out of her hand. It snaked around in demented circles, spewing an icy stream up her entire length. It blitzed her van and sprayed down the driveway. Soaking wet, Holly made a dive for the faucet. That self-defense instructor hadn't exaggerated the effects of a frigid blast of water, she thought wryly. Getting hit in the face was a real shocker.

The whiplashing hose collapsed into a heap of harmless green rubber. Holly snatched up one of the soft old rags for drying the van and she blotted her streaming face. The stranger, she noticed, had stayed prudently out of range. Needing to make certain of what she thought she'd heard, she swung around to peer down at him again.

"Did you say MacKinnon?"

"That's right."

"C-captain?" Her teeth had started to chatter. She could hardly get the word out.

"Uh-huh. I'm usually called Mack." He pushed the gate open and took a step forward. She could hear the gravel crunch under his feet. "Listen," he said, "I didn't mean to startle you."

"Well, you did. We thought you were *dead*!"

Without her glasses she couldn't be sure, but it looked as if a hint of a grin was tugging at the corners of his mouth. "Hey," he protested, "don't sound so annoyed. If you promise not to turn the hose back on, I'll come up there and explain everything."

Before she could object, he suited his action to his words. "The only way you'd recognize my name is if you were part of the class that wrote the letters," he said, mulling it over as he walked. "If I'd realized that, I'd have tried to break the news without handing you such a shock. But, to be honest, I'd been thinking of fifth graders as little kids." He lowered a hand to a height about waist high while a puzzled frown drew his dark brows together. "Which one are you? Let's see; there was Katy and Ingrid, April, Beth and Penny—"

"And Megan," she said a little crossly. "I'm their teacher, Holly Smith. Come on inside, Captain MacKinnon. My students will be tremendously relieved to learn that you're still alive and kicking."

Kicking was right, Mack thought in disgust. He'd just shoved a size-ten boot into his mouth as agilely as if he were a contortionist. "I'm sorry!" he apologized. "The kids mentioned you a hundred times in their letters, but nobody ever told me you looked—"

"Like a fifth grader?"

Mack paused with his foot on the doorsill. "I'd say that we've gotten off to a bad start," he said. "Would it help if I climbed back up the mountain, then came down and tried again? That way, you could keep a tighter grip on the hose and I could try saying something polite. Maybe a few words along the lines of 'How do you do, Ms. Smith? I'm pleased to make your acquaintance.' "

Holly didn't exactly smile, but a dimple flared briefly in one cheek. "Consider it said, and save yourself the walk. Make yourself comfortable, Captain. Let me give you a glass of iced tea. It will take some of the road dust out of your throat while I run up and change into dry clothes."

Following her inside, Mack glanced around with approval. The A-frame really was a cabin, just a single large room on the ground level. Attractively arranged furniture divided the space into areas for cooking, eating, and relaxing. Sunshine poured through the vast floor-to-ceiling windows that drew in the outdoors through both ends of the house.

He lowered the flight bag onto the tweedy couch and then shrugged off his jacket and put it on his bag. Seating himself, he held out his left hand for the frosted drink she offered him.

"Nice place," he commented.

"Thanks. I'm renting it from a friend who's spending a year in Africa as a Peace Corps volunteer. She's due back next month."

The swift, distracted glances Ms. Smith kept darting around the room baffled Mack until he saw her pounce on an oversized pair of eyeglasses. *Blind as a bat*, he concluded, watching the relieved way she shoved them on her face. With eyes like that, they'd never take her in the Marines.

Still barefoot, she scooted up the wrought-iron spiral staircase mounted in a far corner of the room. Heading for the sleeping loft, he assumed. Jamie had mentioned bunking up there in a rollaway bed. The planes of Mack's strong, angular face turned to granite. Poor little kid. Those last four or five letters had sounded increasingly desperate. By the last one, in which he'd scratched out the word *love* and printed *like* in its place, Jamie must have been convinced that everyone he'd been counting on had abandoned him.

In a way, they had. Glowering at the ceiling above

his head, Mack took a swallow of the lemon-flavored tea. But in his case it had been unavoidable. Marines in a war zone laid their lives on the line. It was a heavy job, but somebody had to do it. And the government didn't guarantee you a round-trip ticket when it shipped you off and issued you extra ammo for your M–16.

Teachers, though . . . well, a kid had the right to expect his teacher to stick around. It helped to keep his world from collapsing.

A muscle stiffened in Mack's tense jaw. Holly Smith hadn't done that. She'd walked out on her students without so much as a see-you-later. She'd dumped her responsibilities into another woman's lap, like some faithless wife writing a Dear John letter to the front. He wondered how long she'd been back, and why she'd even bothered to return if she took her duties so lightly.

His resentment toward her had been gaining momentum for six days, ever since that pathetic bundle of mail had finally caught up with him. Reading the cries for help that had traveled halfway around the world and back again had jolted the last missing memory blocks back into place.

Mack had dictated a telegram to one of the nurses, to be sent off immediately. When it came back stamped UNDELIVERABLE, he'd tried telephoning, only to learn that the lines connecting Spruce Ridge with the outside world were temporarily down. He spent the next few days waging a relentless campaign to get himself discharged from the hospital. The doctors weren't keen on letting him go just yet, but Mack hadn't done a fourteen-year hitch in the Marine Corps without learning how to wiggle out of a tight spot.

Once his week's leave was secured, he'd tackled the problem of finding transportation to this out-of-the-way place. It had required more than a little ingenuity. But he'd made it.

I'm here, Jamie, Mack thought. *You counted on me before, and I let you down. Not intentionally, believe me. But I'm here now, and I won't stop looking until I find you.*

Upstairs, Holly traded her cold, clammy clothing for a fresh skirt and blouse, and after unbraiding her hair and combing through the damp, flaxen strands so that they could air dry across her shoulders, she slipped her feet into a pair of summer sandals. When she caught sight of her face in the mirror, she quickly added a touch of lip color.

The thick lenses made her green eyes look huge, and a shadow of worry flickered in their depths. She wished she had time to think things over before going downstairs to face the captain.

At first she had been so overjoyed to learn he was alive that nothing else mattered. But the very next minute she was struggling against the impulse to demand an explanation. What was the big idea, she wanted to ask, of encouraging children to write letters and then failing to drop them so much as a line in response in nearly three whole months? The man's carelessness had had a terrible effect on the children's morale, Jamie's in particular.

Holly's heart ached whenever she thought of that sweet little boy. Every child in the class had loving relatives he or she could count on. All except Jamie. He had absolutely idolized the Marine officer he had never met. For Jamie, the sun rose and set in the East—the Middle East, squarely on top of Captain MacKinnon's head.

Which was why that sudden, unexplained silence had been so devastating. In his letters, the man called Mack had sounded both sincere and compassionate. She had so often read and reread the one he'd sent to her that the page was nearly threadbare. She shook her head, remembering how he had even offered to pitch in financially if Jamie needed money. For a man who had never laid eyes on the boy, the gesture had struck her as being tremendously generous.

But it seemed pretty clear that he wasn't the sort of person she had believed him to be. She and Jamie had both been suffering from an acute case of hero worship, Holly accused herself ruefully. And now they had both been badly disillusioned.

A minute later, from halfway down the winding steps, she caught a glimpse of her visitor. His grim expression startled her. Surely, he couldn't be annoyed because she had excused herself to change out of those sodden clothes. No one could be expected to sit down for a pleasant chat in the condition she'd been in after the hose went berserk!

But, come to think of it, it didn't appear as if a pleasant chat was what Alexander Ross MacKinnon,

Captain, USMC, had in mind. He looked like a warrior about to assault an enemy stronghold.

Holly stiffened her shoulders as she crossed the room to confront him. Spying the light of battle in her steady green eyes, Mack jumped up to return the challenge. They both spoke at once: "Why did you let him down?"

Chapter Three

"Why did *I* let him down?" Holly sputtered. "You've got your nerve, accusing me of a terrible thing like that! We *are* talking about the same person, aren't we? Jamie? Jamie Dawson?"

She saw his eyes narrow. Darts of ebony and gold glinted in their smoky gray depths. Peering up at them was like gazing into the eyes of a wounded, enraged tiger.

"That's right—Jamie Dawson!" he confirmed belligerently. "Don't try telling me you didn't run out on that boy, Ms. Smith. I know bctter. In the last letter Jamie wrote me, he described the way he and the other kids arrived in class one Monday morning to find a substitute teacher waiting for them."

"But didn't he explain—"

''He explained,'' Mack interrupted in a tone edged with flint, ''that everyone he'd ever loved had died. His father. His mother. Lance Corporal Austin Yakich. Granny Sophie. By May, when she passed away, he was firmly convinced that he must be some kind of Jonah. 'Jamie D. the jinx' is what he called himself. A couple of weeks earlier, he had made the decision to stop loving anyone. He was hoping that would keep us safe, you and me. But then you disappeared into thin air and Jamie was positive something terrible had happened to you. And he felt sure he was to blame because he had found it impossible to quit loving you, after all.''

With a moan of distress, Holly sank down onto the couch. The captain's words had hit her like bludgeons.

''They told me Jamie disappeared that night, but nobody ever knew *why*,'' she murmured in a dazed voice. ''I thought that in spite of all our efforts to reassure him, he had been growing more and more despondent about not having heard from you in so long. Also, the specter of a foster home was hanging over his head. The Family Service came to see him and they insisted he would have to leave Spruce Ridge.''

She sent a defiant glance up at the man towering above her. ''But I wasn't about to let that happen. And I assure you, Captain MacKinnon, that I didn't simply run off and abandon my students. Late that Sunday afternoon my brother Gary phoned me. He's an architect who lives down in Palm Springs, California, and he'd just received a hysterical call from our mother.

She told him that Dad had suffered a severe heart attack an hour earlier. The doctors were already preparing him for cardiac surgery, but they didn't hold out much hope for his recovery."

The Marine officer lowered himself to the couch beside her. "I'm sorry," he said, reaching across with his left hand to take her fingers in a firm, comforting grip. "Really sorry. You must have been frantic."

Holly drew a quivering breath as she remembered her panic upon learning that her father was close to death. "I was. He's so dear to me. You feel incredibly helpless at a time like that." She swallowed hard, thrusting down emotion. "Gary told Mother he'd get hold of me and that we'd head for Asheville just as quickly as possible. By the time he called me a few minutes later, he had chartered a private jet and ordered the pilot to start warming up the turbines. He told me to head for Eugene—that's the nearest airport, about a two-hour drive from here. Whoever arrived first, Gary said, was to wait right there for the other. As soon as we joined up, we'd start across country together."

Across country? Asheville? Mack's puzzled scowl cleared when he remembered a little boy's anxious scrawl: *There's a Spruce Pine in North Carolina, where Ms. Smith used to live.* Her voice was pleasantly soft, without any dramatic regional accent, but Mack had known the first time he heard her speak that she wasn't originally from this part of the country.

"Long trip," he commented.

Holly had seen the scowl. In distraction, she pushed a handful of damp hair away from her face. That momentary clasp of his hand had made her hope that he understood. Now it seemed he didn't consider her off the hook yet.

"Yes," she agreed, "a really long trip, even in a jet. And though my brother was starting off clear down in southern California, I knew I'd have to rush like crazy to get over to the airport in time to keep from delaying the flight. There was no chance to pack a bag. I just grabbed my purse and headed for the door. Halfway down the steps I remembered about school the next day, and dashed back inside to phone Timberline's principal. I asked him to please find someone who could fill in for me for a week or so."

Tilting her chin, she met his level gaze unflinchingly. "So you see, Captain MacKinnon, I didn't walk out on my class. There was simply no chance to notify anyone else right then, but Mr. Weems, the principal, knew exactly why I had to leave in such a rush. I don't know how much of an explanation he gave Ms. Crandall when he asked her to substitute, or what she told the children about my absence when she introduced herself the next morning. Probably not much. She would have had her hands full that first day, learning everyone's name and where we were in the various textbooks."

"I guess that would be plenty for anyone to cope with," Mack agreed.

"Tuesday evening my father started to rally. He's

a fighter,'' Holly added proudly. ''I took a few minutes away from the intensive-care unit to phone the Donnelleys. Katy Donnelley was the classmate Jamie was staying with that week. During the long flight back East, I'd had plenty of time to think about the future, and I'd come to an important decision concerning Jamie and myself. I wanted to talk it over with him right away. But instead—''

''Instead, they told you that he had run away.''

''Yes,'' Holly said in dejection. ''By then, they had searched the entire town for him. And questioned all his friends. Finally I called the sheriff's office. Nobody had seen Jamie. And they still haven't. Every law-enforcement agency in the state is keeping an eye out for him. But so far, neither the authorities nor the private detective I hired has turned up a clue as to where he could have gone.''

Mack let his shoulders sag. He looked very tired. And penitent.

''I'm sorry,'' he muttered. ''It seems like I've done nothing except apologize since the moment I first set eyes on you. But I mean it sincerely. I had no right to jump to conclusions about you. All I can offer in the way of an excuse is that I've been swamped by guilt myself where Jamie is concerned. By zeroing in on you, I must have been looking for someone to share the blame.''

His candor won Holly's forgiveness. ''Captain—''

''You'd be justified in tossing me out on my ear,'' he cut in. ''But if you're willing to put up with me a few minutes longer, would you mind dropping the 'Captain' stuff?''

Holly couldn't help remembering how he'd ended his first letter to the children: *P.S. My friends call me Mack.* She should have realized at once that he wasn't a man who cared much for formality. She still had questions to ask him, and serious matters to untangle, but there was no point in being grim about the truce talks.

''No problem, Mack,'' she answered lightly. ''Any friend of Jamie's is all right with me.''

''Thanks, but I doubt that he considers me a friend any longer.'' Mack sucked in a deep breath. ''Time after time he asked me for a favor, a very small one. Just two words—'I'm okay'—scrawled on a card. I never sent that card.'' The wounded tiger's gaze flicked toward her. ''It's my fault he took off. Your not being here to steady him that last morning was just the final straw.''

Holly hadn't been wearing her glasses during that first soggy encounter out in the yard. Without them, anything more than a foot or so away was pretty much of a blur. Later, when she'd marched down the stairs to confront Mack, her indignation had already come to a boil. She'd ignored his appearance and gone straight for the jugular. Now, with the suspicion growing that she might have been as mistaken about him as he'd been about her, she paused to study him closely.

A shallow cleft rescued his rugged chin from implacability, while a rough-and-tumble bump in the middle of his nose eliminated any chance of pretty-boy handsomeness. She liked the dark, level brows above his straightforward eyes. And the short-short haircut suited him rather well.

But Marine regulations alone didn't account for that extreme trim. Holly caught her breath as she glimpsed a semihealed network of surgical scars beneath the close-cropped dark-brown hair on the right side of his head. Her gaze traveled down again, taking in the extra-padded look to his right shoulder. Beneath the loose shirt he wore bandages.

For a moment longer she contemplated the right arm locked in a cast, held immobile across his chest by the sling. Then she looked up and met his waiting gray eyes.

"When did you get out of the hospital?"

As though intending to deny any hint of weakness, Mack's shoulders stiffened.

"At ease!" Holly snapped.

A slow grin, giving her a glimpse of white, even teeth, acknowledged the command. "Aye, aye, ma'am."

Humoring her, Holly thought. Under the weather or not, that docile submissiveness didn't fit the strength of character that seemed an intrinsic element of this military man. Watching the right shoulder gingerly ease back to the support of the couch cushions, she said, "Maybe I should have asked why they *let* you out of the hospital?"

Mack managed a lopsided shrug. "No doubt because

I had turned into such a pest that they figured it was hardly worthwhile keeping me any longer. They turned me loose yesterday afternoon."

"This pest routine of yours—was it something new?"

"Aye, aye, ma'am," he said again, so impudently that Holly pictured legions of doctors and nurses clapping hands to their foreheads. "Up until six days ago, I'd been a model patient."

"I'll bet. What happened six days ago?"

"The mail and my memory caught up with me at the same time."

The hint of laughter lurking around Holly's pretty lips vanished. Shocked, she suddenly noticed the shadows of pain etched into lines around his eyes.

"Your memory?"

"It's been more than a little spotty since the thirtieth of March. According to a sergeant in sick bay with me, that's the day the jeep four of us were riding in hit a land mine."

She longed to know more. Much, much more. But the questions stilled in her throat when she saw the exhausted way he scrubbed a hand across his face.

"It's past noon," she said, hoping to ease the tension by glancing toward the myrtlewood-burl clock hanging on the wall. "How about some lunch? A sandwich and a bowl of soup? Maybe a mug of cocoa to go with it?"

Last night Ms. Smith made me cocoa with marshmelows in it. She said it would give me sweet dreams.

But it didn't. I couldn't stop thinking about that foster home. . . .

Nostalgia flooded over Mack as the snatch of a little boy's letter leaped to mind. Then he blinked, realizing that she had stood up and was waiting patiently for an answer.

"Thanks," he said. "You don't have to do that."

Holly wondered what had caused that wistful expression of his. "I do, unless we both want to go hungry. Compared to the Persian Gulf, Spruce Ridge can't really be called the back of beyond, but there aren't any pizza parlors or golden arches this side of the main highway."

"In that case, I'd be happy to accept your hospitality." As though not quite trusting that distinctly unmilitary timepiece on the wall, Mack glanced at his own watch. "The trucker who gave me a lift up here said he'd be heading down the mountain again at about three-thirty. If I'm out by the road waiting for him, he'll take me back to the bus station in Rainbow where I left my gear."

"That's hours away yet." Briskly, Holly marched off to the kitchen area and opened a cupboard. From the corner of her eye, she watched Mack splay his left hand on the arm of the couch and boost himself up. He stopped as the view through the huge front windows of the A-frame caught his eye.

"I'd swap fast-food places for scenery like this anytime," he said. "In Saudi, I used to dream about returning to the Northwest. I'd conjure up visions of fast-flowing rivers teeming with salmon, mountain peaks covered with pure white snow, and pine needles underfoot instead of that searing sand.''

His tone tugged at Holly's heartstrings. How lonesome he must have been over there, in spite of what he'd told the children about the Marine Corps being his home. In a way, it would have been worse for him than the married men under his command. No warm family homecoming would be waiting for Mack.

Instinct told her he was the sort of man who would hate having a fuss made over him, so she kept her comments impersonal. ''If you'd like to wash up, that flight of steps leads to the loft,'' she said. ''Bathroom's to your left. Help yourself to clean towels on the counter.''

Mack wasted no time in taking her up on the offer. The open spiral stairs felt sturdy in spite of the way they appeared to float upward. At the top he paused to glance around the rustically furnished loft. Braided rugs created warm islands of color against the plank flooring. Stitched in hues of blue, ivory, and maroon, a quilt was smoothed across the twin-sized bed. Half a dozen framed photographs were arranged on the oak bureau.

It was North Carolina more than Oregon, Mack decided. But it was nice. The way she'd combined comfort and beauty to create a look of countrified femininity appealed to him. His gaze swung back to the bureau.

Was one of the photos of her boyfriend? Just because she wasn't wearing an engagement ring didn't mean she wasn't romantically involved. She hadn't been wearing her glasses outside, either, and those seemed to be as essential to her as breathing.

Mack restrained the impulse to sneak across for a closer look at the smiling faces. Instead, he turned the opposite way to enter the bathroom. Closing the door, he chuckled as he saw the height at which the mirror was hung. He'd have a heck of a time trying to shave in that! The oak-framed oval afforded him a perfect view of his Adam's apple. With those oversized glasses balanced on her upturned nose, his hostess reminded him of a little-bitty owl. His grin widened as he remembered the way she'd looked when that whiplashing hose doused her in the face. A cute little owl, with pale, damp feathers and eyes the color of velvet-soft moss.

In the kitchen, Mack's odd reaction to her offer of cocoa caused Holly to fill a glass coffeepot with water instead, and then she placed it on the back burner of her propane stove to perk. Perhaps, she thought, hot chocolate was considered a sissy kind of drink for a full-grown Marine. Opening a can of clam chowder, she dumped it into a pan, stirred in milk, then left it to simmer while she sliced tomatoes and cheese for sandwiches. By the time she heard his descending footsteps, lunch was almost ready.

"Come and sit down." She ladled out two steaming

bowls of soup, then carried them over to the small maple table set with flatware and woven place mats. "What do you take in your coffee?"

"Coffee?" Mack blinked in surprise. "Oh—black will be fine."

Had she misread his signals? He actually sounded disappointed about not having the cocoa. But it was too late now. Watching him grin when he saw that the cup and silver had all been placed to the left of his plate, Holly was pleased that she'd remembered his temporary disability.

"I have to warn you, I'm not a natural southpaw," he said. "I try to spill as little as possible, but by the time I become an expert at eating with my other hand, they'll probably be ready to hack this cast off."

In spite of his disclaimer, Holly thought that he coped very well. She set a slow pace to accommodate his slight awkwardness, and couldn't help feeling gratified when every morsel of food vanished.

"That was really welcome," Mack thanked her afterward. "Much different from the MREs, I assure you."

"No kidding?" she teased. "I thought for sure that those Meals Ready to Eat would have been one of the highlights of your stay in the exotic Middle East. Along with mysterious veiled women, of course, and camels jogging across the sand dunes behind pickup trucks."

For the first time in far too many weeks, Mack found himself laughing spontaneously. "Being there was an experience, all right, but not one I'm in any hurry to repeat. Saudi came as a bit of a culture shock, even to old hands like me.''

''How old?'' she was horrified to hear herself blurt.

Mack didn't take offense. ''My age, you mean? I'm thirty-two, with fourteen years in the Corps.''

Definitely a career man, Holly took note. What, she wondered, did he look like in dress blues? Pushing the intriguing image away, she asked, ''You enlisted right out of high school?''

''The week after graduation. After a couple of years in the ranks, the powers-that-be came to the conclusion that I showed leadership potential, and they sent me to Officers' Training School, in Quantico, Virginia.''

A bit of background he'd revealed in a letter to her students popped into Holly's mind:

Spruce Ridge sounds like the little town in Washington State where I grew up. We had a sawmill there. Plus plenty of trees and a lot of rain. . . .

''Long way from home,'' she commented.

''Not as far as the Persian Gulf,'' Mack pointed out. ''Some of the men had trouble getting acclimated to that place, especially the part about weekend passes that didn't include wine, women, and song. Alcohol is taboo in Arab countries, you know, and the women were strictly off-limits.''

Holly dimpled. ''Then all that leaves is song. With such deprivation to lament about, it sounds as if they'd have the basis for a classic country-western number.''

"I can almost hear them twanging it in Nashville now." Mack was clearly enjoying the repartee. "What kind of lyrics could be written about a lady who looks much too young to be a schoolmarm leaving her old folks at home in North Carolina, and heading out West to teach in Oregon?"

"Something Stephen Foster might have put to rhyme," Holly bantered in return. "All about a twenty-six-year-old spinster who decided it was high time she spread her wings. But I doubt that Willie Nelson or Dolly Parton would be interested in setting a dull yarn like that to music."

As she threw back her head to laugh, the burl clock crossed her line of vision. Time was flitting past. He would have to leave soon, and there was so much she wanted to ask him. Things she had to know for her peace of mind.

Hastily, she stacked the dishes in the sink. Then, leading the way back to the couch, she motioned her guest to sit down again. But after they were comfortably seated, she didn't know where to start.

The things the Marine captain had spoken of concerned harsh realities. A military man was trained to confront the enemy. To someone like Holly, who went out of her way to avoid antagonizing butterflies, it sounded like a terrifying prospect. She doubted that she could ever summon the courage to stand her ground against danger, the way he had done.

"You . . . you lost your memory?" she plunged in at last.

"On the eighth of April, I woke up aboard a hospital ship. I'd been completely out of my head for more than a week," Mack said quietly. "A corpsman told me what my name was. That matched the dog tags around my neck, so I figured he must be right. One of the men I'd been out on patrol with was there in sick bay next to me. His leg was in traction. He told me he'd been driving the jeep during the explosion. I'd been sitting behind him."

"What about the other two men with you?"

The slow shake of his head was as mournful as taps at a funeral.

A small sound of distress escaped from Holly's lips.

"It was almost like hearing a radio announcement about some tragedy that befell a group of strangers," Mack continued after a short, painful silence. "Alexander MacKinnon was as much of a stranger to me then as those other three men. The doctors aboard ship said not to push it, that the amnesia was a natural result of my crack on the head, and chances were that my memory would gradually return."

Holly looked up, unable to keep from focusing on the scars beneath that close-cropped hair. Chills skittered up her spine.

"Did it?" she whispered.

"Not fast enough to suit me. Every now and then I'd get flashes of a Cub Scout hiking through a forest or of a teenager playing basketball, and I knew that kid had been me," Mack said. "That started after I was flown to a military hospital in Germany where surgeons specialize in patching up head wounds. While they were at it, they operated on my shoulder, rearranged three or four ribs, and aligned the bones in my arm again so I'd have full use of it someday. Once I could be moved, they shipped me home to Washington State.''

That was standard procedure, he explained. Whenever possible, injured military personnel were assigned to care facilities in or near their home state, to make family visits more convenient.

''Since I'd grown up in a town called Shelton, right on Puget Sound, they transferred me to the huge Naval hospital in Bremerton to finish recuperating,'' Mack went on. ''That was late last month. By then, I was able to fill in most of the details of my early life, and I didn't have any trouble recognizing my sister when she came to see me.''

The information that he had a sister gladdened Holly's heart. Mack wasn't completely alone in the world, after all. ''How wonderful!'' she said.

''Mmm. Would have been even better if I'd been able to tell her who Jamie Dawson was.'' Mack used the tone of one tacking bad news onto the good tidings he'd spoken of earlier: ''He was named as my beneficiary on the government life-insurance policy I'd filled out at the end of February. Arlene had been sent the papers for safekeeping.''

''Jamie?'' Holly said. ''*My* Jamie?''

''Your former student,'' Mack subtly redefined her description of the boy. ''Yeah, that Jamie. It nearly blew my mind when I read the name on that long printed form and tried to figure out who he was. All I knew was that he must have been someone I cared a great deal for if I was leaving him money in case—well, in case I didn't come back."

He almost *hadn't* come back, Holly remembered. If he'd been sitting on the opposite side of that jeep. . . . She pushed the dark thought aside and grabbed a deep breath. "Were Arlene's feelings hurt that you hadn't named *her* as beneficiary?"

"No, of course not. She's already more than financially secure. She's a highly successful commercial artist and heads up a company that handles the graphics for a lot of business firms around the area. Leo, her husband, is a dentist with a flourishing practice. They have a nice home and a boat. It won't be a strain for them to put their two daughters through college when the time comes."

"Did you say something about your mail a little while ago?" Holly asked.

"While I was being transferred around, so were my personal possessions, and also the mail that kept accumulating after the jeep blew up. It stayed one jump behind me until six days ago, when it finally caught up. The rest of my missing memory links fell into place when I sat down to read six months' worth of letters."

"You had kept them?" Holly asked in surprise. "The ones from last year too?"

In reply, Mack unzipped the flight bag he'd brought with him. As he pulled out a thick wad of letters, she spotted two airmail envelopes addressed in her own neat handwriting among the children's penciled scrawls. The postmarks ranged from the previous September right up to a date in late May. It was the day after she flew to Asheville, Holly realized. It was also the day Jamie disappeared.

"So this is what brought you here!" she exclaimed.

Mack nodded. "Minutes after reading that last group of letters from Jamie—which I'd never seen before—I shot off a telegram to him saying 'I'm okay.' It was returned marked 'undeliverable.' Then I tried to contact both you and the town doctor by phone. The operator told me that all lines into Spruce Ridge were down."

"A ferocious thunder-and-lightning storm crashed through the mountains last Tuesday," Holly explained. "It struck transformers and turned telephone poles into toothpicks. The whole community was without power or phones for days."

"When I stopped to consider the matter rationally, I figured something like that must have happened," Mack admitted. "But lying there in the hospital, my patience went up in smoke and I wanted out. Finally, just to get rid of me, they cleared me for a week's leave and showed me the door yesterday afternoon. I've been traveling ever since—by plane, taxi, and bus."

"And logging truck," Holly put in. She could feel for those hapless hospital administrators who had tried to hold him back once he'd decided to get himself released. It would have been like pitting a skateboard against a tank.

"What an odyssey!" Admiration for his doggedness was clearly evident in her smile. "Mack, I'm sorry you've had this long trip for nothing. Go on back to the hospital and finish getting well. Just give me your address before you leave. I promise to notify you the very instant Jamie is found."

His cold look was fair warning that her suggestion clashed with his own ideas. "What if that never happens?" he asked. "You said yourself that the sheriff's department has spent nearly three weeks on the case already. If neither they nor a private investigator have had any luck in that long period, it seems to me that it's time someone who really cares about that boy took over." He waggled the packet of letters in front of her face. "There are enough clues in here to make me feel confident of being able to find him myself. And when I do, Ms. Smith, I'm going to file for immediate adoption. I want Jamie for my son."

Chapter Four

"Adoption?" Holly cried. "But you can't!"

"Watch me!"

They were leaning toward each other, nose to pugnacious, bumpy nose. "Mack," she said, scooting back in a dignity-restoring movement, "that's a wonderful and generous gesture, but it isn't necessary, not in the least. Before lunch, I mentioned coming to a decision regarding Jamie and myself while I was flying back East with my brother. That was what it involved. After thinking it over thoroughly, I made up my mind to adopt Jamie myself."

"*You*? That's ridiculous!"

Holly jumped up off the couch, wadded up her fists, and knuckled them defiantly at her hips. "What's so ridiculous about it?"

Mack made a belated effort to douse the green fire blazing in those eyes of hers. "Hey, cool down. I didn't mean to hurt your feelings. It's just—" He gestured vaguely around the cabin. "Well, for one thing, this place isn't big enough for you and a growing boy. Besides, it isn't even yours. You said yourself that the friend you're renting it from is due back from Africa next month."

"So?"

"So where would you put Jamie?"

"I'll find a place. A nice place."

"How are you going to support him? You called yourself a spinster. That means you're a single girl, right?"

"A single *woman!*"

"I beg your pardon. A single *woman*. Either way, you don't have a husband."

Holly gritted her teeth. "I don't need a husband to help me support one little boy."

"Oh, sure, I forgot, schoolteachers are well-paid professionals. Their salaries range right up there with rock stars and computer geniuses, I'll bet."

"What about Marines?" Holly countered hotly.

Mack puffed out his chest. Regrettably, the sling supporting the heavy plaster cast kept anyone from noticing its formidable dimensions. "What *about* Marines?" he challenged.

"I suppose they get paid real great."

"Pretty darned good, yes. On top of my regular

salary, there's also eight or nine months' worth of accrued combat pay tucked away.''

''How could I have forgotten?'' Holly drawled caustically. ''You didn't have any wine or women to squander it on in the Persian Gulf, did you? Tell me, what's going to happen next time there's an international incident?''

''We'll do a good job,'' Mack promised. ''But if you're referring to me personally, I'm due to be bumped up to regimental level. As soon as I finish convalescing, I'll be taken out of the field and reassigned Stateside to planning and operations duties.''

''Congratulations,'' Holly said in a ho-hum tone. ''I suppose a boy of eleven could manage alone all day while you're off planning and operating. But just in case they decide to reassign you off to Timbuktu, what'll become of him? You're single too, remember? You don't have a sweet little wife to stay back at Camp Lejeune or Camp Pendleton or Camp Whatever-It-Is that you're currently calling home, and keep her eye on a little waif you decided to adopt on the spur of the moment.''

''That decision wasn't made on the spur of the moment,'' Mack growled. ''I gave it a lot of thought.''

''Well, think again,'' Holly advised, ''because it isn't going to happen. The minute Jamie is found, I'm petitioning the court to let me have him. They will too. I'm far more suited to be a parent than you are.''

''Ha!''

They had reached a stalemate. Both of them realized

that bravado wouldn't further their cause another inch. Warily, they eyed each other.

"*You* don't know where he is," Mack pointed out.

Holly's gaze fastened on the letters he clutched. She wished she had X-ray vision. "Jamie *told* you where he planned to go?"

"Not in so many words. I figured it out for myself, reading between the lines. The only thing is. . . ."

She eyed him suspiciously. "The only thing is *what?*"

"There's a small problem with transportation," Mack was forced to admit. "I can't drive with this cast on my arm."

"Don't tell me a handy logging truck won't drop you off at wherever-it-is?"

"It's mean of you to be so sarcastic, especially since I was about to suggest a compromise."

"What sort of compromise?"

"We go together. You drive," he added with a notable lack of enthusiasm, "and I'll supply the directions."

"A partnership?"

Holly mulled it over. Not a bad idea, all things considered. On occasion, two heads really *were* better than one. Grudgingly, she admitted that Mack seemed to believe in people pulling together for a common cause. He'd written something to that effect in a letter to Jamie:

Teamwork is real important when you're in the Marines. The other men and I are all part of platoons and companies. That way, we can count on each other when the going gets tough. . . .

"It might work," she allowed. "Provided no one holds back information or tries to steal a march on the other guy."

"Agreed."

"Decisions are to be mutually arrived upon," she stipulated. "And all expenses divided fair and square. Right down the middle."

"Fine with me."

"What about when we find Jamie? What will we tell him?"

Mack liked the fact that she had said "when we find Jamie," not "if." "We'll tell him that we both love him and that each of us is anxious to adopt him. We'll leave it up to him to decide which of us he wants as a parent."

Nothing could be fairer than that, Holly supposed. "Poor kid," she said. "He won't find that an easy choice to make."

Trying to remain impassive, Mack set out a proviso of his own. "This deal is strictly between you and me," he warned. "I'm not sharing my information with any private eye. Jamie was scared stiff of being hauled off to some foster home. If he caught wind of a stranger getting too close, he might take to his heels again."

"This investigator is discreet. He doesn't sport a

badge on his chest, or drive a car with flashing lights on the roof.''

''Think that would cut any ice with Jamie? A detective's likely to be a detective, so far as he's concerned.''

''The man's had a lot of experience.''

''And Jamie's still missing.''

It was a telling point, and one to which she had no rebuttal. Unreasonable or not, her adversary had just put his finger squarely on the bottom line.

''As I see it,'' Mack went on when she remained quiet, ''a personal approach is called for. The two of us can team up and look for him together. *Or,* you keep right on waiting for your Rent-A-Cop to pull a rabbit out of the hat and I'll go by myself. Which will it be?''

He wasn't going to budge an inch, Holly thought with glum certainty. If he walked out that door, she'd never see him again. More to the point, she might never see *Jamie* again.

She held out her hand and nodded. ''All right, we'll do it your way. Naturally, if I'm to chauffeur you around, I'll expect you to behave like an officer and a gentleman.''

''Naturally.'' Mack liked a good loser, and he kept a poker face as he engulfed her small hand in his big left paw. ''May I assume that my chauffeur will be both an exemplary driver and a perfect lady?''

''Count on it!'' she growled. ''Now, if you'll kindly release my hand, I'll go telephone Mr. Gordon.''

Firing the private investigator, however, proved to be a more complicated task than Holly had expected.

"What do you mean, my services are no longer necessary?" the raspy voice on the other end of the line demanded. "Did the kid come home by himself?"

"No, but that isn't the—"

"Sounded to me, when you contracted for those services, that you were mighty attached to that youngster, Ms. Smith. That you were concerned about his welfare."

"I was and still am."

"Then what's the idea of throwing in the sponge? I've barely had a chance to start my investigation."

Being interrupted not once but twice honed a sharp edge to Holly's comeback: "You seem to be quite a slow starter. In nearly three weeks you've reported no progress whatsoever!"

Pete Gordon hadn't expected a lecture from a female client, and his tone turned bluff and conciliatory. "There, there, little lady. These things take time."

Holly clenched her teeth. "You've *had* time!"

"And made good use of it. I've put out feelers all over the place," the detective blustered. "Showed that photo of the boy around every bus station, fast-food joint, and video arcade within a wide radius. Say, I even dressed in shabby old clothes, makin' like I was just another homeless bum, and went nosin' around the shelters. The drifters who hang out at those fleabags are not exactly eager to talk to strangers, but I got my ways of finding out what I want to know."

Holly experienced a wave of revulsion. That callous attitude probably went along with his profession, but somehow she hadn't pictured the process of finding somebody as being so cold and insensitive. She had a sudden vision of Jamie being collared by that hard-edged man, and then interrogated and browbeaten.

The unsavory notion stiffened her resolve. "You're off the case, Mr. Gordon," she said crisply. "I intend to search for Jamie myself with the help of another of Jamie's friends. Thanks to him, new information has just come to light. We expect it to lead us to the boy in short order."

"Now, look here!"

"No, *you* look here," Holly shot back, tired of this paper tiger's insolence. "As of this moment I am terminating our arrangement. Kindly make out a final statement and issue a check to cover the unused portion of the retainer I paid you. I'll expect them both in the mail on Monday morning!"

At first, Mack's fingers had itched to snatch the phone away from this civilian, take charge, and tell the surly investigator, whose bluster was clearly audible from where he stood, to— Well, the temptation was great, but Mack was shrewd enough to hold his fire. Holly Smith had agreed to team up with him and leave her hired gorilla out of it, but that merely showed her deep concern for Jamie and not any great confidence in Alexander MacKinnon.

He felt like cheering when her patience snapped and

she began standing up to the bully. In spite of her petite size and soft-spoken ways, that woman had a lot of backbone, he decided. With growing admiration, he listened to her refusal to be bulldozed into letting Gordon stay on the case. It was clear to him that the private eye had simply been wasting her money. Now she seemed to have come to the same conclusion and was putting an end to the joker's freeloading ways.

Mack wondered where she'd scraped up the cash to pay the man that retainer she'd mentioned. From what he'd heard, private eyes charged an arm and a leg. Her life-style wasn't austere, but she didn't look all that well fixed, either. On a schoolteacher's salary, she couldn't have afforded an expense like that for very long.

As the telephone connection was severed with a resounding bang, Mack swallowed a grin. "Sweet fellow," he observed blandly. "Hired him for his sunny nature, did you?"

Holly shot him a jaundiced look. "I hired him," she announced, "because his secretary is the younger sister of a good friend. Krista assured me that Mr. Gordon had twenty years of experience in tracking down juvenile runaways."

"Oh, I get it. A bounty hunter."

She wondered how many Marine captains wound up being throttled by civilians. A goodly number, she wouldn't be surprised.

"A *specialist!*" she snapped. "When I phoned from Asheville to ask if he would take the case—"

"You mean you never even *met* this gumshoe?"

"*Gumshoe!*" she exploded. "Where did you get your vocabulary—out of a time capsule? That word went out with the last Humphrey Bogart movie!"

Mack chuckled. "You're forgetting Alan Ladd."

Holly maintained control with a colossal effort. "As you have deduced," she informed him through clenched teeth, "I hired Mr. Gordon sight unseen. Once I returned to the West Coast, I did confer with him in person in his office in Eugene, but our original contact was made over the phone. From Asheville. While my father's life was still hanging by a thread. Tell me, what would *you* have done in my position?"

An embarrassed flush reddened Mack's deep, desert tan. He remembered the fierce sensation of helplessness that had assailed him when he lay in that hospital bed, reading and rereading Jamie's long-delayed letters. And his miserable frustration when the telegram was returned. And his bitter chagrin on being unable to contact anyone in Spruce Ridge by phone.

"I don't see what else you could've done," he admitted quietly. "I'm sorry, Holly. Sorry for shooting off my big mouth. Sorry it cost you so much to get nowhere. I hope this is the last time I find myself apologizing to you. If we're going to be partners, we have to quit jabbing at each other. We need to pull toward the same goal or it simply won't work."

"I know," she agreed, suddenly ashamed of her own obstinacy. "We can't hope to find Jamie if all we do is feud. For his sake, I'm willing to call a cease-fire, and stick to it.''

''Fair enough.'' Mack dropped the letters back into the flight bag and then collected his belongings with one-handed efficiency. His eyes met hers as he turned toward the door. They weren't angry anymore. Just determined. ''Time to get going,'' he said. ''I'll grab a lift down the mountain with the trucker, and as soon as I collect my gear from the locker where I left it, I'll hop a bus over to Eugene or Springfield. Somewhere near the interstate, anyway. Let me give you a call this evening, after I've found a place to stay. We can arrange when and where to meet tomorrow morning. I don't want to waste any time getting started on our search.''

''Neither do I,'' Holly assured him. ''But I'd like to make an alternate suggestion. Let me walk out to the road with you while we toss it back and forth.''

It sounded to Mack that she'd meant what she'd said about calling off hostilities. Since his hand was full, he let her hold the door for him. ''What do you have in mind?''

She stepped out onto the porch behind him. ''There were fourteen kids in the class that wrote you those letters, Mack. Thirteen of them still live right around here. Those boys and girls would be very disappointed if they learned you came to Spruce Ridge and didn't give them a chance to meet you. So would their parents.''

''I remember every one of them. My only excuse is

that a bad case of tunnel vision has been cracking the whip over me for the past few days.''

He stepped down onto the gravel path. Turning, he faced Holly before she, too, could move off the porch. It was an interesting sensation to stare straight across into those big green eyes of hers that were usually a foot beneath his. From this angle, she looked mighty grown-up.

''I'd be disappointed not to meet them too,'' he said. ''How do you figure I could manage it?''

''By letting me arrange a potluck dinner. I know it's on the spur of the moment, but the pastor of the church down in the village is always glad to lend his basement to any group needing a place to meet. It's sort of an informal community center, and plenty large enough to accommodate a big crowd.''

Mack had never kidded himself that he was anyone special. Her use of the word ''crowd'' came as a surprise. ''Do you think people would turn out at the last minute like this?''

Holly gave an emphatic nod. ''Mack, you panicked a whole townful of people when you stopped writing so suddenly. Every single one of them will want to see with their own eyes that you've actually come home safely.'' For a second or two, her glance strayed to the yellow ribbon tied around the maple tree. Quickly, then, it zoomed back to corral his gaze. She hoped that the droopy thing had escaped his attention.

''At this short notice, we'll probably wind up eating a lot of different macaroni or tuna casseroles,'' she warned. ''Things made with fixings folks keep on hand. But I think you'll be surprised at what a warm welcome goes along with that down-home food.''

A smile lifted his mouth as he heard that folksy expression. ''Down-home food is my favorite kind,'' he assured her, wondering what had made her take that quick, sneaky look at the tree. He had seen the yellow ribbon fluttering in the breeze when he walked down the road to her cabin. It was just a symbol, of course, and nothing he had any right to take personally. More than once, Jamie had mentioned those ribbons in his letters. ''But what happens later?'' he asked Holly in a practical tone. ''Don't tell me there's a Holiday Inn around this neck of the woods?''

''No, they're every bit as scarce as pizza parlors in Spruce Ridge,'' she told him. ''But plenty of people in town have spare rooms, and I know that every one of them would be delighted to put you up overnight. In fact, there would probably be a lot of competition for the pleasure of your company. Whoever wins would want to take you off to church with them in the morning too,'' she added. ''Services are over by midmorning, though, and right afterward we could head for Rainbow to collect your gear and get started on our search. What do you say?''

''I say 'thank you very much.' It sounds like a fantastic suggestion.''

Mack's eyes shone with suspicious brightness. Suddenly, Holly wanted to hug him. She knew it had never occurred to this amazingly modest man that he was regarded as a hero by the citizens of this tiny community. She just hoped that strong left hand of his didn't get totally wrung out by the end of the evening.

"Great!" she replied, hauling herself up short before she made the mistake of getting overly sentimental. Captain Alexander MacKinnon had come to Spruce Ridge for one reason, and one reason only, she reminded herself sharply: to find Jamie Dawson. Which was her goal too. Unfortunately, once he was found, they both couldn't keep him. Truce or no truce, that fact was bound to make them enemies in the long run.

"Go ahead," she urged Mack. "Flag down that trucker when he comes by. Tell him you won't need a lift down the mountain, after all. I'm going to form a telephone committee to call everyone in town."

By five o'clock they were headed toward the village. Strapped into the comfortable bucket seat on the passenger side of the Ford Aerostar, Mack kept a prudent eye on Holly's driving techniques. Within a few miles, after noting the competent way she handled the wheel, his skeptical look faded. He glanced back, making sure that the cardboard box stashed in the rear wasn't sliding around.

Earlier, he had watched Holly remove hot dogs and buns from her freezer and then stow them into that box with a bag of potato chips and a six-pack of cola.

"Food after my own heart!" he'd remarked. "But somehow, I pictured a schoolteacher pushing healthy veggies at the kids on every possible occasion."

"That's what they have parents for, remember? There are plenty of times when food is almost like medicine. Really essential, when someone has been sick and needs to get well again." Holly had reached for a package of paper napkins to toss into the box. "Fortunately, tonight everyone is going to be eating for fun."

Then she marched out of the kitchen, leaving Mack standing there with a bemused expression on his face. It had sounded to him as if Ms. Holly Smith were speaking from experience.

He now gave himself a shake. Why should he care? Her personal life was none of his business. In fact, the less he knew about Ms. Holly Smith's past, present, and future, the better off he would be. They had agreed to a partnership, not a friendship. Just as well too. Sometime soon, their tug-of-war for the affections of a little boy was going to start. She wouldn't budge. And he had no intention of giving an inch. As sure as shootin', the two of them were going to wind up enemies.

That night, Holly had trouble falling asleep. It had been a jam-packed day, full of hefty emotions and promise for the future. Captain MacKinnon had made it safely home at last. Tomorrow, the two of them were going off in search of Jamie. The outlook seemed brighter than it had been in weeks.

The impromptu potluck hadn't damaged anyone's morale, either. The event had been wildly successful.

Family after family had crowded into the church basement, eager to meet the Marine captain whose letters and gifts from the other side of the world had given each one of them a special stake in Desert Storm.

In her sleeping loft, Holly snuggled more deeply into the cozy quilts. Mack had been great with them all, she thought. He had patiently answered every question asked of him. And he'd held out his left hand again and again to accept the clasp of a well-wisher. Laughingly, he made up a children's game to decide which family would have the honor of hosting him overnight. Zach's little brother was the winner, and almost reeling from fatigue, Mack had accompanied the Swensons home, calling back over his shoulder that he'd see Holly in church the next morning.

She drifted off to sleep with the memory of his tired smile lingering in her mind. Sometime afterward, a sound awakened her. Jolted out of the depths of slumber, Holly couldn't pinpoint what sort of noise it had been. Not then, at least. She only knew that it had been clearly audible in the midnight stillness.

Rigid, she listened, grateful that there was no sense of another presence within her cozy A-frame cabin. But the billowing curtains reminded her that the front window was wide-open.

The sudden roar of a powerful engine growling to life out on the road catapulted her from bed. Running barefoot across the plank floor, she peered into the night. Too late. All she could make out was a pair of rapidly vanishing taillights.

Seconds later the red glow faded, leaving the night tinged only with the silver radiance of a quarter moon. Not until then did Holly realize that it was the closing of a car door that had yanked her from sleep.

The door had closed ever so quietly. Still, the inevitable clash of metal against metal had been enough to rouse her.

With a gasp, Holly went flying back across the room to snatch up her glasses. Relief flooded over her when she directed her flashlight downward and saw the blue-and-silver Aerostar still safely parked in the shadows of the driveway.

Two baffling questions ruffled that sense of relief, however. If it hadn't been a car thief after her van, who *had* stopped out there on the road?

And why?

Chapter Five

Mack was highly trained in discreet surveillance, and he spotted Holly slipping into church mere seconds before the opening psalm. He watched her muffle a yawn behind the hymnal, and observed her determined struggle to stay awake during the sermon.

With a resolute effort of his own, Mack riveted his gaze on the pulpit. This was hardly a pious way for him to spend a Sunday morning. He tried to decide at which of them he was more irritated—at Holly for looking like she hadn't gotten to bed until dawn, or at himself for letting it bug him. And for wondering who had kept her out so late.

Trying to be fair, he reminded himself that dating on Saturday nights was a time-honored American custom. Just because he had been out of circulation recently didn't mean that other red-blooded men weren't eager to escort an attractive blonde for the evening. Yesterday afternoon he had elbowed his way into the schoolteacher's life without a moment's advance notice. What he ought to be doing was thinking of a way to thank her for putting a busy social life on hold to arrange that party in his honor last night.

What a *terrific* party! The entire population of Spruce Ridge must have turned out for the impromptu affair, Mack realized. Still uncomfortable with his role as a local celebrity, he concentrated on how much he had enjoyed meeting those kids. He'd sure had fun linking up smiling faces with names at the bottom of letters. Their genuine affection had gone a long way toward softening up his tough leatherneck hide.

He should have been satisfied with that. So why, Mack grumbled silently, couldn't he keep his eyes from drifting across the aisle to the pew where a young woman sat blinking sleepily behind big round glasses?

Walking down the church steps at Holly's side after bidding farewell to the entire congregation, Mack did a fair job of concealing his peevishness. "You look," he remarked, "like someone who could use a second cup of coffee."

"I never even got the first one," Holly confessed. She rubbed her droopy eyes as she unlocked the van. "It's only thanks to that shrewish alarm clock of mine that I'm out of bed at all. What a night!"

These artless comments hardly sweetened Mack's

temper. His annoyance deepened as he settled himself in the passenger seat. "Well, I'm glad you had such a good time."

His resentful tone went right on past Holly, who was sneaking in another yawn behind her hand. "I sure did," she said. "That was one of the great spur-of-the-moment potlucks of the world. You made at least a hundred new friends last night, Mack. I never saw anyone hit it off with a crowd like you did."

Who could sulk after such an accolade? Mack gave a reluctant chuckle.

"They *were* wonderful," he said, "every single one of them. The only trouble was, I ate too much. And then this morning, Mrs. Swenson forced a huge platter of Swedish pancakes down my throat. Didn't give me any choice about eating them."

"Sure, sure, she hovered over you with a rolling pin. I know."

Awkwardly, Mack dragged the seat belt across his middle. He was grateful that Holly let him cope with the clasp himself, even though they could probably have gotten started a minute and a half sooner if she had lent a hand. "What time did you leave?" he asked, trying to sound casual.

"About half an hour after you did. Kevin and Moose helped me collect all the aluminum cans for recycling. Then I drove home to shampoo my hair and pack a suitcase. Though you'd never know it to look at me, I got to bed reasonably early. But after being awakened like that, I wasn't able to get back to sleep until almost sunrise.''

Mack's rancor evaporated with a jolt. ''What happened?'' he asked.

Rather than answer at once, Holly drove the van out of the church parking lot and through the length of the town, all three blocks of it. Just outside the city-limits sign, she pulled into a turnout and cut the engine.

''I didn't like to talk about anything upsetting back there where all the Sunday strollers could hear,'' she said. ''About last night, I don't really know what happened, just that the sound of a closing car door woke me up around midnight. But whoever was driving took off down the grade before I could make it over to the window.''

As he remembered the isolation of her house, a stirring of close-cropped hair prickled at the back of his neck. ''Was there any attempt to break in?''

''Not that I could find. My first thought was that car thieves were after the van. There's no garage, you know, and it sits out all the time,'' she added uneasily. ''But it was still locked when I checked the door. Mack, can you think of any reason for that disturbance?''

Hearing the strain in her voice, he wished he had a simple, reassuring answer to give her. For a change, a company of two hundred and thirty men wasn't depending on him for survival. This was just one schoolteacher, who was probably worrying about nothing. He would have given a lot to brush her worries aside with a few comforting words, but that would have been as worthless as a Marine nurse's trying to ease the pain of his injuries with a placebo.

"Why would anyone have stopped on the road outside your cabin last night?" he asked, mentioning the logical answer to her question. He shook his head. "Holly, I don't know. It doesn't make sense, particularly if they were headed downhill. Anyone who wanted to pull over and light a cigarette or adjust his rearview mirror would have picked that nice flat plateau above your place to stop."

Oddly enough, Holly found it comforting that he didn't attempt to make light of her concerns. Captain Alexander MacKinnon might be a stubborn Marine whose objectives conflicted with her own plans, but he wasn't about to brush her off with a phony explanation. Never would he have said, "There, there, little lady," and expect her to take it kindly.

Suddenly, she was very glad she had elected to depend on Mack instead of on the detective who had proved so ineffectual. "Well," she said while she started the van again, "it's over, gone and forgotten. Let's go pick up your gear. With any luck, there'll be a ladies' room at the bus station where I can change out of these Sunday clothes. And it would sure be marvelous if they had some sort of miracle machine that dispenses caffeine by the quart. After that. . . ."

"After that," Mack said, filling in her questioning pause, "we're going to find Jamie."

* * *

The Rainbow bus depot had the somnolent air of a place that hustled once a day and then subsided into a torpor. While Mack retrieved his duffel from the locker, Holly lugged her suitcase into the women's room and changed into a cool, comfortable sports outfit. Then, in the waiting room, she dissolved her morning drowsiness in coffee. Lots of it.

"As you may have noticed, I've been living up to my part of the bargain by staying under the speed limit and avoiding accidents," she reminded him when the luggage had been stowed and they were back in the van. "I believe that supplying directions was to be your responsibility?"

"Yup," Mack agreed. "Up there at the blinking light, turn left onto 126."

Tamping down her impatience, Holly followed orders. Sooner or later, she assured herself, he was going to have to break down and share his inside information with her. Unless, of course, he broke their pact. But she didn't believe he would act so dishonorably, not even if by doing so he could be sure of getting to Jamie first. In the interests of a harmonious trip, therefore, she bit back the impulse to demand a few solid specifics.

Westbound, the two-lane, cross-state highway seesawed up and down, following the course of the McKenzie River. After staring moodily out the window for a few miles, Mack straightened up with a puzzled observation.

"I haven't noticed any no-hitchhiking signs. If this were Washington or California, they'd be posted all over the place."

"It's not, though," Holly said with a slight smile. "Oregon has its own way of doing things."

Mack's interest centered on how that state's laissez-faire attitude might affect their quest. "Hitchhiking's legal here?" he asked. "So the cops wouldn't have automatically picked up Jamie if they caught him standing alongside the road with his thumb out?"

"Not for hitchhiking, but truancy is against the law here, same as anyplace else. Three weeks ago, when Jamie disappeared, school was still in session. Chances are, any patrolman spotting a youngster thumbing a ride when he should have been in class would have stopped to ask questions. But that didn't happen."

"Have you any idea what he took with him when he left?"

She had already answered this question for the police, and again for the private investigator. "Except for his bike and a few sets of clothing, most of Jamie's things were kept in a storage cabinet at my house. I checked it carefully when I returned from North Carolina. His backpack and an old sleeping bag were missing, along with a coat he'd worn last winter. He also took along a collapsible fishing pole and a sturdy pair of hiking boots."

Jamie, thought Mack, had made some pretty self-sufficient preparations for a cross-country hike. If he had taken care to avoid main roads and population centers, that could explain why nobody had noticed the boy. Mack drew his level dark brows together in a frown. "Are you saying he broke into your cabin while you were gone?"

"No, of course not. Jamie wouldn't do anything like that. After Granny Sophie was taken to the nursing home, I gave him a key. That way, he could come and go whenever he wanted. The cabin was sort of a haven for him during those musical-chairs weeks while he was staying with the other children. I think he spent so much time with me because he was afraid of wearing out his welcome with the parents of his classmates."

To Mack, it sounded as if Jamie had always felt assured of a welcome at his teacher's house. And that was great for Jamie and generous of Holly. She had taken on the role of mother to the boy when he had nobody else to turn to. But a kid that age needed, above all, a father to help him along the road to becoming a man.

"What else did he have with him?"

Holly suspected that Mack's gruff tone was a cover-up for emotion. Though worried about the missing boy, he seldom brought his feelings out in the open. In fact, he had come right out and admitted this in a letter that Jamie had proudly shared with her:

You bet I meant it when I signed my letter with love. That isn't a word I've had a chance to use much in the past. But coming from me to you, it's straight from my heart. . . .

Holly wondered if Mack ever loosened up with anyone. So far, he hadn't mentioned a girlfriend, and that seemed amazing. She would have thought that a tall, good-looking man in uniform would be irresistible to the ladies.

Probably it was just as well he was sitting over there dressed in ordinary civilian knockabout clothes, she told herself. It would definitely be a mistake for her to get attracted to him. The only thing that the two of them had in common was a bone of contention.

"He took along clothes, sneakers—and a toothbrush, I hope," she answered Mack's question. "Not his bike. Jamie left that behind at Katy's house. He probably had a little money left from Granny Sophie's last Social Security check. But aside from the things I've already mentioned, there were only the last few watercolors his mother had painted."

"I hope he's been able to keep them safe," Mack said. "Judging from the one he sent me, they were pretty special."

There was pain in his voice and a drawn expression around his eyes. Remembering back a few years, Holly recalled how easily one tired when recovering from a long siege of illness. The past few days must have been very hard on this man, she thought. Worrying about Jamie. Battling to secure his release from the hospital. Traveling by any and all means though he was far from strong.

"I didn't think to mention earlier that the backseats of the van fold down," she said, rather too casually.

''I can rearrange things in just a few minutes if you'd like to stretch out for a short rest.''

Mack's chin gave an implacable tilt. ''Thanks,'' he growled. ''I wouldn't.''

Men! Holly thought in disgust. ''Are you always such an ornery beast?''

A hoot of laughter defused his huffy indignation. ''I hope not. Let's just say that for the past six weeks I've had about all the lying down a man can take.''

''I know just how you feel. Being an invalid gets wearing real quick. But what would you suggest I do if you should suddenly fold up on the floorboards?''

''Ignore me? Just keep going?''

''I could,'' she said sternly. ''Provided I knew where we were headed.''

''That's easy. Just put on the brakes when you see the Pacific Ocean.''

''Look,'' she snapped, ''this partnership wasn't my idea. If you've changed your mind about sharing your deductions with me. . . .''

''Whoa!'' Mack pleaded. ''I didn't mean to sound uncooperative. An officer and a gentleman never goes back on his word. To tell the truth, though, I feel a little embarrassed. My deductions aren't what you'd call carved in stone. In fact, they're pretty much guesswork. Would reading Jamie's letters yourself convince you that I'm strictly on the level?''

Holly took her time about answering. Trust was a fragile thing, she knew, and she already repented her flare of temper that had backed him into a corner. And she needed no further assurance that he was an honorable man. Though they had been acquainted for only a short time, Captain Alexander MacKinnon's integrity had shone through loud and clear in his every letter to her students. Instinct told her that he would stand by any promise he made, regardless of the consequences.

"That isn't necessary," she replied at last. "Those letters were personal, strictly between Jamie and you." A boy needed that man-to-man closeness, she thought. Then she pushed away this notion, because it hurt to acknowledge such a home truth. A moment earlier she had slackened speed, but now she increased her toes' pressure on the accelerator. "Vague or not, why don't you tell me just what Jamie said to convince you he was headed toward the coast?"

Ms. Holly Smith was really something else, Mack marveled. Though he had a pretty well-developed sense of fair play, he wasn't positive he would have had the moral fiber to make the decision she had just made.

Jamie, of course, had known what sort of woman she was. After the poor kid had convinced himself that he was a jinx to everyone he held dear, he'd done his best to stop loving her. But he hadn't been able to. Throughout the letters, Mack had discerned a deep affection between the boy and his teacher.

Acknowledging the closeness between the two of them left him feeling morose. For the first time, he wondered if he was doing the right thing in trying to claim Jamie for himself.

The silence inside the van drew into a tense, expectant vacuum, waiting to be filled. Mack leaned back and eased his body's aches with the headrest and cushions. He wished that the doubts filling his mind could be so simply assuaged.

"In one of his early letters, Jamie told me that Granny Sophie had taken to calling him Warren," Mack said. "It didn't bother him too much, because Warren was his grandfather's name, and he assumed that she was thinking of the good old days. So was he, Jamie told me. But he had his own ideas about what it constituted." Mack went on with a quote from a letter: " 'The best old days was when me and my Mom lived at the beach for a whole summer. Here is a picture of a wild flower she painted there.' "

"The beach," Holly groaned. With a sinking heart, she considered how much territory that took in. To say the least, it was an obscure clue.

"There's more," Mack assured her quickly. "Not much, but a little. Jessie—Jamie's mom—must have been quite a talented artist. He told me that the reason he had so few of her paintings left was that they sold very quickly. Let's see if I can remember the way he put it. 'The lady at the craft store always wanted a whole bunch. I heard her tell my mom once that tourists who come to the beach on vacation bought them quicker than she could hang them up.' "

Holly caught her breath. "This saleswoman is a wonderful lead. The place Jamie remembered from his good old days must have been quite a tourist center. If we can just find that craft store—''

She broke off, looking appalled. The magnitude of the task seemed to loom as high as Everest.

Mack's wry tone echoed her reservations. ''Good trick if we can swing it,'' he agreed. ''Oregon's coastline stretches for hundreds of miles, and it's dotted with towns, each one probably a mecca for summer visitors. How many artsy-craftsy gift shops do you suppose we'd find if we started counting?''

''Don't ask,'' Holly groaned. ''Are you sure he just called her the lady at the craft store? Not Mrs. Whosis who runs the Starfish Souvenir Stand in Newport? Or Southbeach? Or Pacific City?''

''Dreamer,'' Mack chided. ''In his very last letter Jamie referred back to where he was going again, but I'm afraid that what he said isn't going to be much more help. He said that some other kid could have his place in the foster home, and that he was leaving to find the good old days.''

''What a job we have ahead of us!'' Holly murmured. ''Look, Mack, traffic is really picking up, and I need to concentrate on staying on the right road. Keep your eye out for road signs, would you, please? We'll let Jamie's clues simmer in our heads until we can really focus on them.''

An overpass carried them across I–5, the wide, fast freeway that started down in California at the edge of the Mexican border, arrowed straight through the length of Oregon, and then spilled on into Washington and continued clear to the Canadian border. At least an hour was needed to make their stop-and-go way through the metropolitan sprawl comprising Springfield and Eugene.

By the time traffic thinned, they were both starving. As Holly spotted a taco stand, she started to slow. Then she glanced dubiously at her companion.

Mack shook his head in regret. "My left-handed efforts with a taco or burrito would embarrass both of us, I'm afraid. Let's try and find a place with food that can't get away from me so easy."

"How about some take-out chicken? I see a place up ahead."

"Suits me fine."

The hot food buoyed their spirits while it filled their stomachs. Holly took out her wallet to pay for the meal, hoping that Mack remembered their agreement to divide expenses equally.

He didn't raise a fuss. However, when they got back into the van, he remarked that the gas gauge was getting low. "I'll take care of that," he said. "Next time we'll do it the other way around. A deal?"

"A deal." Holly had been dreading the nuisance of nickel-and-dime accounting, and his suggestion seemed a good means of keeping things simple. But when she angled the van up to the pumps at a gas station, she had a hunch he was feeling frustrated by the cast on his arm. He was just macho enough, she reminded herself, to resent having a woman get out and manipulate the gas pump while he sat by and watched.

She gave him a reassuring smile. "Remember what I told you about Oregon having its own set of rules? One of them is that the service station attendants, not the customers, pump the gas."

Wearing a greasy cap that proclaimed *Orrie's Full Serv,* a gray-bearded man puttered over to fill the tank with unleaded. Mack handed him some cash to cover the bill. "How far are we from the coast?" he asked.

" 'Bout sixty miles." The attendant took his time counting out the change. "That's to Florence, mind. The ocean is a mite farther, out beyond the dunes."

"Dunes?" Holly repeated curiously.

"Oh, yes, ma'am. That part of the Oregon coast is famous for its sand dunes, didn't you know? Movie companies come up from Hollywood all the time to film their desert scenes there. It's something to see, I guarantee it."

"Thanks, we're looking forward to it." Holly was only mildly interested. She had more on her mind than the expectation of finding some movie crew out on location. But as she reached to switch on the ignition, she caught sight of Mack's jubilant expression.

"Why the grin?" she asked. "You look as tickled as if he just handed you a winning lottery ticket with your change."

"I was thinking of how Jamie ended one of his letters to me. He said: 'Whole big Oregon sand hills of love.' "

''Mack, what a fantastic clue! Probably neither of us would even have seen its significance if it wasn't for Orrie back there at the gas station. Come to think of it,'' she added, ''I've read that the Oregon dunes are quite spectacular. Even so, I doubt Jamie would have used an expression like that unless those big Oregon sand hills were something he'd seen himself.''

''In fact, I have some proof that those dunes were an important part of Jamie's good old days. Look!''

Mack had been sharing his legroom with the battered old flight bag containing the packet of letters. Now he bent down, tugged at the zipper, and removed a small framed painting. He waited until Holly pulled over in front of a pet-supply store and then he handed it to her.

It took her a moment to understand his elation. At first, all she noticed was a watercolor painting of a dainty wildflower. The artist's signature, Jessie Dawson, was airily brush-stroked in one corner.

Looking up in bewilderment, she saw the sparkle in Mack's eyes, and took another glance. This time she spotted it.

It wasn't the flower he wanted her to look at but the dun-colored background.

''The dunes!'' Holly exclaimed. ''Jessie's wildflower was painted somewhere near the dunes!''

Chapter Six

With a definite goal to aim for, their task seemed less Herculean, and Holly indulged in the pleasant fantasy that Jamie would be sitting cross-legged on the first dune they spotted. He would recognize the van right off, of course, and come running with open arms to show how overjoyed he was to see her again. Naturally, he'd be glad to meet Mack too. She swallowed hard. Naturally.

Gazing out his own window, Mack missed the shadow flickering across Holly's features. He had been drinking his fill of the verdant countryside. During those endless months in the Middle East, he had felt a stab of loss every time he compared that sere landscape with the breathtaking greenery of his native land.

Now he was home and thanking God to be here in one piece.

Not everyone had been so fortunate. His still-healing wounds were a vivid reminder of the others who hadn't come back. He had spent weeks mourning the pair of Marines under his command who hadn't survived the explosion, and also wondering if, as their superior officer, there was any way he could have prevented the tragedy. Common sense told him there wasn't. It had been chance. Bad luck. War.

With humble gratitude he blessed the quirk of fate that had led him to sit on one side of that jeep rather than on the other.

Just beyond the highway, a broad, blue reservoir shimmered in the sunlight, and Mack feasted his eyes on it until the water was no more to be seen. As he turned to comment on the beautiful sight to Holly, a dazzling glint reflected in the van's side mirror caught him square in the eyes. He winced at the bright, blinding glare caused by sunlight striking the windshield of another vehicle back on the road, and he bent swiftly to rummage in his flight bag for a pair of dark glasses.

The abrupt movement caught Holly's attention, and glancing across at him, she smiled and said, "You're looking better."

His heart was touched by the gladness in her tone. "I *am* better," he declared, almost reluctant now to put on the glasses and screen the uncomplicated pleasure he glimpsed on her face. "Thanks for worrying about me back there. I must have sounded like a real grouch.''

''That you did,'' she agreed. ''But I'm afraid that both Dad and my brother would have acted the same way.''

''You mentioned that your father suffered a heart attack. Is he coming along okay now?''

''He's making a marvelous recovery. Dad's a building contractor, and I'm afraid he's already itching to be back at work. But for the family's sake, he agreed to relax at home this summer. No worrying about blueprints or building codes for several months.''

After crossing the Suislaw River a while later, they pulled over and got out to stretch their legs. They found the ten-minute break most welcome. Once Mack had his seat belt refastened, Holly eased the van back out into the westbound lane. As he turned his head for a last glance at the river, his eyes were dazzled by a familiar glare in the side mirror. It was too familiar a glare, and he murmured, ''Strange.''

Holly was alerted by the taut wariness in his tone. ''What's strange?''

''Miles back I was half-blinded by the dazzle of light against a particularly high windshield.'' Mack tilted his head, avoiding the incandescent blaze in the mirror. ''Now there's that same vehicle, hanging the same distance back.''

Holly darted a glance into her own side mirror. ''Looks like one of those oversized pickups, the kind with the supermacho tires that boost the rig high above the rest of the traffic on the road. Are you sure it isn't a different truck? The one you noticed earlier should have passed us while we were stopped there beside the river."

"I'm sure. Try picking up the pace and see what happens."

As Holly bore down on the pedal, the speedometer shot up and the reflection of the big pickup dwindled to toy size. Then it seemed to expand, once again filling the mirror with its hulking mass.

"He sped up too," she said nervously.

Mack hadn't missed the truck's unsettling maneuver. In spite of the sun's bouncing off the broad windshield, he kept a vigilant watch on the oncoming truck, wishing he now had the superb pair of smoked goggles that the Corps had issued him to be worn in the desert beneath his kevlar helmet. And he wished as well for the M–16 that had always been within reach. Apprehensively, he hoped that there would be no need for a weapon.

They flashed past a small white sign on the side of the road. "Speed zone. Slow down," Mack warned. "Little town just ahead."

The village of Mapleton was even smaller than Spruce Ridge, with the no-frills atmosphere of a logging community that Holly knew so well. But never had anything looked so welcome. She jerked the wheel and veered out of the traffic lane to a curb fronting a café-bookstore. She caught her breath as the pickup roared past aggressively, and then she expelled it with a startled whoosh as the blatant rumble of engine noise smote her ears.

"Mack!" she cried in alarm. "That's exactly the same uproar I heard on the mountain road outside my cabin last night!"

The truck that sped past them had been a Dodge Ram, painted a malevolent black. Its mud-splashed license plate worried Mack far more than the size, sound, or color of the vehicle that had come within inches of bulldozing them off the road. Maybe sloppy maintenance was responsible for the illegible state of the numbers, he told himself. Just like the driver *might* be a muscle-flexing showoff with more than a few cans of beer under his belt. Then again, maybe not.

But what would a trucker have against them? Mack made no effort to figure out an answer just then, because the fear in Holly's eyes was of much more concern to him at the moment. He twisted, intending to give her a comforting hug, only to be stymied by the seat belt and the heavy cast binding his right arm to his chest.

"It's okay now," he said reassuringly. "You can relax, Holly. He's gone."

"Thank goodness!" Boy, she was such a coward, Holly lamented. The danger was past, yet her voice sounded as if she were operating a jackhammer.

Mack released the catch of his belt with a snap. "Come on," he said, pointing to the café. "Coffee-time. My treat."

He was nice, Holly thought, feeling the inner quaking start to ebb. Deep, down-to-the-bone nice. It must be obvious that she was a total chicken, scared into a blue funk by a pushy, roadhog driver. Yet there he sat, offering coffee as matily as if she'd been a fellow hero.

"Thanks," she said, "but could we make it tea instead? My nerves are ready for soothing, not any more jangling."

"Herb tea it is," Mack said gravely.

By the time they finished the short drive into the town of Florence, they both agreed it was too near closing time, even for the shops that might be open on a Sunday, to do any canvassing that evening. Instead, they decided to look for a place to stay. But this objective was thwarted again and again by signs indicating that the lodging places they passed were full up.

"Looks like we may finally have hit it lucky." Mack indicated a motel up ahead, and on its facade trembled a red neon *Vacancy*.

At once, Holly flipped on her turn indicator and made for the entrance. But inside, at the registration desk, disappointment awaited them.

"There's one queen-size left," said the desk clerk, a young redhead wearing a badge marked *Ruthie*. She pushed the register toward them.

"Wait a second," Holly protested.

Beside her, Mack shook his head as he said, "We need two rooms."

Ruthie shook her head too. "If it wasn't for a last-minute cancellation, that sign out front would have been turned off an hour ago. This time of year, we're almost always full up by the middle of the day.''

''Great for you, but tough on us,'' Mack observed. ''Unfortunately, we didn't have time to make reservations. We're searching for a lost youngster, and chances are pretty good that he's someplace in this area.''

''I sure wish you luck,'' Ruthie said sympathetically. ''I doubt you'll find anywhere to stay along the main drag tonight, though.''

''Could you recommend an alternative?'' Holly asked.

''How about a bed-and-breakfast? A friend of my aunt's runs a nice little inn a few miles below here on the Coast Highway. Want me to call Mrs. Dillon and see if she has a couple of rooms you can have?''

''We'd sure appreciate it.''

Soon afterward the van was headed southbound on 101. High, undulating ridges of sand lay off to the right. Beyond the hills they caught occasional glimpses of the rugged seacoast.

Holly eyed the picturesquely rippled slopes in amazement. ''This looks more like North Africa than North America. It wouldn't surprise me a bit to see a Bedouin caravan plodding across those dunes.''

Mack nodded. ''I'll bet they'd feel right at home here, especially if they stuck to using camels, those reliable old ships of the desert, and left behind those fancy new pickup trucks the government issued them.''

As soon as the words ''pickup truck'' were out of

his mouth, Mack had the urge to bite his tongue. Blast! Why did he have to go and remind her of that frightening experience? Since leaving Florence, Holly had stopped acting as if she expected to see a powerful black hobgoblin every time she glanced in the rearview mirror. Now he noticed her fingers tighten over the steering wheel as if she were holding on for dear life.

Resolutely, however, she refrained from mentioning the scary incident that was on both their minds. "If Ruthie's directions are right, we ought to be spotting the Dunescape Inn pretty soon," she said instead.

"Sounds like an appropriate name, don't you think?" Mack marveled at the vistas sculptured by sand and wind. "I wonder how much farther down the coast these dunes extend."

Upon their arrival, they were dismayed to learn that the sand hills ranged for more than fifty miles along the central Oregon shoreline. As Holly and Mack exchanged stunned glances, she bit back a groan. Fifty miles! It would be a tremendous area to try and search!

The inn's owner told them that access to the dunes was quite limited. Dune-buggying was a popular pastime down at Hauser on the southern end of the stretch, and the nearby town of Florence offered a handy entrée if people just wanted to walk for a short distance across the shifting sands.

"A few trails lead down from the bluffs," Phoebe Dillon added, referring to the high headlands overlooking the sea south of her inn. "There's also a public road from the state park out to a jetty, if you're interested in fishing. Be mighty careful of the fog, though. It's been known to billow in without warning, damp and dangerous and as thick as pea soup.''

Holly shivered at the eerie picture these words conjured up. How easy it would be to get lost out there! To pitch straight into the unknown, or be swallowed up by the unexpected.

Both fascinated and repelled, she gazed through the wide parlor window at the constantly shifting scene. Sweeping inland from the edge of the surf, the sand resembled an amorphous body of fluid movement.

``Our dunes are absolutely unique,'' Mrs. Dillon said, as proudly as if she had ordered them out of a catalog for her guests to enjoy. ``In some spots the formations rise as high as two or three hundred feet above the ocean. Some folks say the rivers cause them, washing sediment down from the mountains to hurl into the sea. The surf grinds it up and spits it back, for miles inland in many places. Here and there, whole spruce-pine forests are swallowed up by the sand. Nothing like it anyplace else in the world, or so I've heard tell.''

Holly had never happened across a similar phenomenon. Following her hostess up a carpeted stairway, she did her best to shrug off the jittery feeling those humpbacked waves of sand gave her. How soon, she wondered, would they encroach upon this sturdy beach house and swallow the veranda plank by plank?

The innkeeper opened a door at the end of the hall. ``I hope you'll find this to your liking,'' she said.

''You'll be sharing a bath with Mrs. Cramer on the other side.''

Having once lived in a college dorm, Holly wasn't ruffled about this arrangement. Not even a confirmed nitpicker could have found a flaw in the delightful guest room into which she was ushered. Starched eyelet curtains draped the window and canopied the four-poster bed. Luxuries abounded: a vase of tiny pink rosebuds, elegant and glossy travel magazines, padded hangers. A plush robe snuggled along the foot of the bed, and an enameled tray held hand-dipped chocolates in fluted white paper cups.

''How grand!'' Holly opened a drawer of the carved chest. ''Umm, lavender sachets. You've thought of everything!''

Phoebe smiled at this tribute to her hospitality. She was a big, capable woman in her early sixties, as comfortably upholstered as the furniture in her front parlor.

''People come a long way to stay with me, and I like having things just so for them,'' she said. ''Your young man will have the large guest room downstairs. A soldier in the war, was he?''

''Marine.''

''Thought so. No mistaking a military man. Beautiful, that straight, proud bearing of theirs. His room has a cozy gas fireplace to ward off the chill,'' Phoebe went on. ''The damp seeps in of an evening here by the ocean. With him being hurt and all. . . .''

''He'll love it,'' Holly assured her. ''But the fact is—''

A telephone bell jangled, sending Phoebe off with an apology. Holly stood looking at the closed door. "The fact is," she said, making the point unmistakably clear to herself if to nobody else, "that Captain MacKinnon is *not* my young man!"

A lavish breakfast was served to the guests at the Dunescape Inn. It was a good thing, Holly and Mack later agreed, because after that, the day went downhill fast.

After driving back to the small coastal city of Florence, they began canvassing every gift shop, craft store, and art gallery in town. Wherever they went, Mack asked to speak with the owner or manager. Then he would display the exquisite little painting Jamie had sent to him.

"Jessie Dawson was the artist," he said. "Have you ever carried her work?"

"No," the proprietor of a beachfront boutique replied. "But if the price is right, I'd sure like to. Customers love bringing pretty souvenirs like this home from vacation."

Variations of this answer were repeated up one street and down another. "Lunch break," Holly announced finally, and she crooked her finger to lure Mack inside a charming café redolent with the zesty tang of oregano. Basket-covered Chianti bottles sat atop red-and-white checkered tablecloths, their glass necks collared with melted candle wax. Helping themselves to bread sticks, they studied the menu.

Later, slanting discreet glances at him, Holly was cheered to see that Mack handled his plate of ravioli as if he'd been eating with his left hand all his life. She twirled linguine around her own fork, her thoughts reverting to the frustrations of the morning.

"Everyone who looks at Jessie's painting loves it," she mused aloud. "You'd think someone would remember that airy technique of hers."

"Not if they'd never seen it before. This isn't the only tourist center along the dunes coast," Mack reminded her. "But each little shop is a new possibility. All we can do is keep on with the process of elimination."

"Sure, I know. Sooner or later we're bound to get lucky."

"You bet," he said staunchly. "At least we don't need to worry about finding a place to stay. I'm sure glad we decided to use the inn as our base of operations, no matter how far the search takes us."

"Me too. Isn't Phoebe a gem?" Across the table from him, Holly had a sudden vision of Mack relaxing beside the fireplace in his room, basking in its warmth. Doggedly, she pushed the image aside and unfolded a map of the area. "How about trying the Old Town district next?"

But Old Town shopkeepers were of no more help than their counterparts in the modern sector of Florence had been. At six they gave up and returned to the bed-and-breakfast.

"We've made a great start already." Mack's spirit-lifting tone caused Holly to reflect on what a terrific morale builder he must have been for his company of Marines. "Tomorrow, maybe we can set out in the other direction. But for tonight, how about putting our main concerns aside and having a leisurely dinner somewhere?"

"Sounds good." Holly followed him up the steps of the Dunescape Inn and greeted their hostess, who was enjoying a brief rest on the veranda. "Hi, Phoebe. Can you recommend someplace nice to eat?"

"Lovely seafood at the Sandy Scupper a mile down the road." Phoebe spotted the small painting Mack carried. "Bought yourself a souvenir, did you?"

On impulse, he handed Phoebe the dainty watercolor to inspect. "No, actually we're using this to try and find a young boy. He and his mother spent several months in this area two or three summers ago. Jessie Dawson sold her artwork through a local craft shop, and Holly and I figure that if we can find the right shop, it might lead us to Jamie."

Phoebe studied the painting with a thoughtful frown. "Pretty little thing," she remarked. "Can't help thinking I've seen something like it before."

"Where?" Holly asked eagerly.

"That's hard to say. Hanging on a wall somewhere. But I don't think it was in any store." Phoebe handed back the watercolor. "Let me cudgel my brain. Sometimes, if I sleep on a puzzler, I wake up with the answer next morning."

Hoping that that would be the case this time, Holly and Mack separated to get cleaned up.

An hour later they entered the seafood restaurant their hostess had recommended. The chinook salmon they ordered had been caught that afternoon just offshore, and served with dill-sprinkled vegetables, it was as delicious as it was fresh.

Holly sat back, and after another sip of Riesling, she said, "No wonder Jessie Dawson spent a whole summer here."

"Unfortunately, we don't have that long. At least I don't," Mack modified his statement. "I'm out of the hospital on a short leash, remember?"

"Oh, Mack, we're sure to find Jamie . . . well, any day now." Holly tried to sound optimistic. "What happens next with you? I know you have to be back within a week, but I'm talking about later, when the doctors say you're in perfect health again?"

"I'll have thirty days' accrued leave coming. Vacation time," Mack elucidated with that half-teasing grin Holly found so attractive. "Afterward, I head for California and report to Camp Pendleton."

"Not far from Disneyland. Lucky you!"

"They tell me there's also a promotion in the works," he added in a modest tone.

"You'll be a major? Congratulations!" Holly accompanied her good wishes with a warm squeeze of his hand. "That means gold oak leaves on your shoulders, doesn't it, in place of your silver bars? Will you be living right there on base?''

''I suppose so.'' The considering look on Mack's face told Holly that he hadn't thought that far ahead as yet. ''It's not mandatory, of course,'' he added. ''I could easily rent a house or apartment in a regular neighborhood. But that means commuting—a waste of time and gasoline. To be honest, there has never been any reason up until now to consider establishing quarters elsewhere.''

Slowly, Holly withdrew her hand. ''Up until now?''

Avoiding her eyes, Mack made an awkward gesture. ''Well, it depends, doesn't it?'' he asked uncomfortably. ''On what Jamie decides.''

All the joy seemed to siphon out of the evening as Holly remembered their pact. Jamie was to choose which of them he wanted as a parent. Either Mack would be the boy's adoptive father, or she would petition the court to become his new mother. They couldn't have it both ways.

''Sure,'' she replied stiffly, opening her purse to take out enough cash to cover her share of the meal. ''I guess that *is* what our housing arrangements depend on. We're sort of in the same boat, actually. I'm also going to have to decide what to do about a new place to live.''

Later, as they walked out to the parking lot together, Mack told himself that his pact with Holly was working out just fine. Countries made these short-term treaties all the time. It was a handy way to protect themselves from a common enemy, explore a chunk of outer space together, or wage a desert war. Afterward, unfortunately, when allies no longer needed each other's assistance, hard feelings were apt to arise. From the way Holly jammed the key into the ignition switch and slammed the gearshift into reverse, he had a hunch that this mutual-aid alliance of theirs was starting to deteriorate ahead of schedule.

They had lost track of time at the restaurant, and this end of the Sandy Scupper's parking lot was nearly empty. After noting that there were no other cars around when she exited the restaurant, Holly had let her usual vigilance slip for just a second. Rather than easing down on the accelerator pedal, she floorboarded it as she swung around in reverse.

Purring at the unexpected chance to show off its horses, the obedient engine powered the Aerostar into a rubber-burning arc. The swing culminated in an abrupt thud as the bumper encountered the hulking metal dumpster at the far edge of the lot.

Holly's first contrite thought was for her passenger, and she cried, "Mack! Are you all right?"

"Yeah. Fine." He slanted a sideways glance at her, and then shook his head. "I hope we can say the same for your car."

A hasty examination showed that the dumpster had absorbed the impact without so much as a crease. The van's bumper had not fared so well, however.

"Oh, no!" Holly was torn between shedding tears and kicking herself in disgust as she surveyed the once-smooth curve. A two-foot length of the bumper had crumpled in the impact. Its formerly glossy platinum hue now bore hefty dents and splotches of ugly green paint where the dumpster had apparently punched back in retaliation.

"You don't do things by halves." There was a sternly repressed undertone of amusement in Mack's comment. Their eyes met for the first time in five minutes. "Feeling better, now that you've got that out of your system?"

"Uh-huh. That'll teach me, won't it?" Holly cast another lamenting look at the bumper. "Mack, I apologize. I never lose my temper. Never! And to have done it behind the wheel of a car is inexcusable. You could have been badly injured!"

The amusement vanished as Mack's thoughts inevitably focused on what had happened a few months earlier, when a vehicle in which he'd been riding had flipped out of control.

"We're both lucky not to have been hurt, Holly," he told her. "The bumper can be straightened out or replaced, and we're okay. Maybe this experience will teach us both not to let our emotions get out of hand."

Their sobered mood lasted all the way back to the Dunescape Inn. But as they climbed the steps of the veranda, the setting sun drove all petty concerns from their minds with the splendor of its departure. They lingered side by side, watching the fiery clouds blaze and then cool to indigo. The sun became a glittering memory on the vast horizon as it hoarded its final beams to warm the ever-shifting hills of sand.

"Sometimes the beauty of the dunes holds me almost spellbound," Holly murmured. "And sometimes they make me afraid. They're so stark and uncompromising. A truly hostile environment if somebody—especially somebody little—were lost out there among them."

"He isn't." Firmly, knowing full well what she was talking about, Mack turned her to face him. "Jamie's been here before, remember? He had months to grow accustomed to this shoreline. He knew what he was coming back to."

Holly swallowed, aware of the rise in her spirits. Slowly but surely, her morale rose beneath his sensible persuasiveness. "That's true," she agreed. "And he's awfully resourceful."

He nodded emphatically. "There was one of his letters where he told me about handling the chores. It's hard to believe the stuff a ten-year-old kid could manage to cope with. He wrote me about it after Granny Sophie was taken off to the rest home. I think Jamie was trying hard to convince himself that what had happened was for the best."

Jamie had never told anyone else about that, Holly thought. Tears prickled in her eyes. She blinked them back so he wouldn't see them glinting in the fading light. Jamie had loved his Marine pen pal so much that he had trusted him with his deepest secrets.

Gazing down at her shining blond head, Mack was remembering another part of that same letter:

At first I was real mad at her and the doctor. I told them to go away. I said we didn't need them around. But I guess that wasn't really true.

Yeah, Jamie had needed Holly all right, Mack told himself miserably. Not him. All he had been able to do back then was write letters. He'd had to count on other people to help the boy he was coming to love so much. It was Holly whom Jamie had needed then. But what about now?

"Don't get discouraged," he told Holly. "We'll find him."

She bobbed her head, but kept it bent. "Of course we will."

"Part of me wants that so bad." Mack reached out with his good hand to brush aside the silken curtain of hair and caress her throat. "And part of me wishes it wouldn't happen just yet."

Holly couldn't keep her head bowed any longer. She looked up, eyes drenched with confused tears, to meet his gaze.

Why? she was about to ask. But the question died in her throat. Partly because she already knew the answer. Partly because her own feelings were shredded by an identical turmoil. Partly because his lips, soft and warm as that last burnished dune, had slowly lowered to press against hers.

Fleeting paradise.

Too soon—much, much too soon—Mack straightened up. As he squared his shoulders, she thought that his military bearing had never been more in evidence.

"Because when it does," he said, answering the question she'd refused to ask, "everything is going to change between us. Isn't it?"

Once again, sadly, she nodded. Her eyes were dry now. And determined.

"Yes," she whispered. "Yes, I'm afraid it is."

Chapter Seven

"Knew I hadn't seen that picture at any shop," Phoebe crowed the next morning. Triumph tinged her smile as she circled the table, filling coffee cups with a rich, aromatic brew. "It's hanging in Clara Fosdick's sun-room. Must have caught my eye last spring, when I went over there to collect the slips she promised me from her prize geranium."

Mack abandoned his cheese omelet. "Can you find out if your friend's picture was painted by the same artist?"

"Already did." Phoebe set a basket of piping-hot blueberry muffins in front of her guests. "I gave Clara a jingle this morning while the oven was heating. Hers is signed Jessie Dawson, same as yours."

"Phoebe, you're a wonder!" Holly exclaimed.

The innkeeper took the compliment as her due. ‘‘Figured you’d want to know where Clara had bought it,’’ she went on. ‘‘The back of her painting has a sticker on it, identifying the shop. Sunset Moods, the place is called. It’s off the Coast Highway just down past Glenada.’’

Holly remembered a dot marking the tiny town of Glenada on her map, and she jumped up from the table so fast that her napkin slid to the floor. ‘‘That’s not far from here!’’

‘‘Barely a hop, skip, and a jump. There’s no need to rush.’’ Breakfast was a hallowed ritual at the Dunescape Inn, and Phoebe wasn’t about to let her guests skimp on what she considered the most important meal of the day. ‘‘Sit down and finish your melon, young lady. Give this man of yours a chance to tuck a nutritious plate of food under his belt before you two go galloping off.’’

Tactfully, Mack pretended not to see the rosy wave of color suffusing Holly’s cheeks. He assumed that their traveling together had led to the misunderstanding by their hostess, who, judging from the bookcases in the parlor filled with sentimental novels, was a romantic at heart. He saw no reason to disillusion her by insisting that he and the pretty blond schoolteacher were merely part of the same search party.

After a sip of orange juice, he teased Phoebe with his smile. ‘‘Do you by chance have a relative named Inga Swenson who lives up in Spruce Ridge? Nice lady, and makes great Swedish pancakes, and never lets anyone leave the table until they've devoured several helpings.''

''We aren't related, just kindred spirits,'' Phoebe sassed. ''Eat that omelet before it gets cold.''

Listening to their good-natured banter, Holly decided with relief that Mack hadn't even noticed Phoebe's embarrassing slip of the tongue. Drat people who jumped to conclusions! She'd done her best to explain that there was nothing personal between herself and Mack, but the woman hadn't seen fit to listen.

Her cheeks grew warm again as she remembered last night's kiss on the veranda. It was the setting, she felt sure, that had inspired that unexpected moment. The glorious sunset, the tang of faraway places wafting across the ocean on the salty breeze, the cry of gulls heading home to their mates—all had combined to work their magic. But his comment about everything changing as soon as Jamie was found had left Holly with no illusions. Their alliance was temporary, a convenient example of teamwork and nothing more. For the sake of her future morale, she needed to keep that fact firmly in mind.

Perched toward the front of a craggy precipice, the craft shop had an impressive setting, but Holly and Mack ignored the view and hurried inside. The walls and showcases of Sunset Moods displayed a large variety of artwork and handicrafts, but to their acute disappointment, the proprietor glanced at Jessie Dawson's watercolor without so much as a flicker of recognition.

"Sorry, I'm not familiar with this artist's work," he told them. "However, we do have many other beautiful paintings to choose from."

"Yes, I can see that," Holly replied distractedly. "But—"

Mack stilled her protest with a touch. "Remember what Jamie said in his letter? That his mother had sold her paintings to the *lady* at the craft store?"

After introducing himself as Loomis Tugman, the proprietor told them that he had owned the shop for only about a year and a half. He went on: "When Etta Silverstone decided to retire, I bought Sunset Moods from her. These days she spends most of her time down in Arizona. Not during midsummer, of course," he added, upon glimpsing their crestfallen expressions. "Could I ask why you wanted to see her?"

"Ms. Smith and I are trying to locate a missing person," Mack said. "It's possible that Mrs. Silverstone would be able to help us. Can you tell us how to get in touch with her?"

After thinking the matter over, Mr. Tugman apparently decided that they looked trustworthy, and he offered to telephone the former owner of Sunset Moods to see if she would be willing to speak with them.

Forty-five minutes later they were ringing the doorbell of a double-wide coach in a large, well-kept mobile home park farther down the dunes coast.

Traces of potter's clay speckled Etta Silverstone's

fluffy white hair, and smears of acrylic paint gave her smock a cheery, Jackson Pollock look. The peppy seventy-year-old seemed pleased to welcome guests.

"Loomis tells me you're looking for someone," she said after ushering them into a living room that overflowed with the evidence of several busy hobbies. "Sit down, won't you? I'll be happy to help if I can."

Within a minute, tears had sprung to her faded blue eyes. "My, this takes me back! I'd recognize those delicate brushstrokes anywhere." Nostalgically, she gazed down at the small framed painting Mack had handed her. Then she glanced up in distress. "Oh, but my dears, if Jessie Dawson is the one you're hoping to locate, I'm afraid the quest is futile. I heard in a roundabout way some time ago that she's no longer living."

"We know," Holly told her. "It's Jessie's little boy we're trying to trace. Jamie's great-grandmother died this past winter, and she was the last relative he had. After staying with friends almost until the end of the school year, Jamie disappeared. We think he ran away because he was worried about being placed in a foster home."

"Oh, good gracious!" Mrs. Silverstone exclaimed.

"Jamie looks back on that summer he and his mom spent at the seashore as a wonderful, carefree experience," Mack took up the explanation. "We believe that he might have tried to recapture that former happiness by coming back here."

"Anything's possible." The elderly woman eyed her

visitors guardedly. ''You'd be from one of those agencies, I suppose? Child welfare or some such?''

''No, ma'am,'' Mack said with an emphatic shake of his head. ''Holly was Jamie's fifth-grade teacher, and they're very devoted to each other. He and I became pals through letters we wrote back and forth while I was stationed in the Persian Gulf. The last thing either of us wants is to see that boy living among strangers. In fact, we're both anxious to adopt him.''

Beaming her approval, Mrs. Silverstone relaxed. ''Jamie was a charming little boy. I'm delighted to hear that the three of you mean to become a family.''

Holly opened her mouth to deny that any such arrangement was intended. She subsided into silence upon catching sight of Mack's warning glare.

Giving no indication of conflict between Jamie's two would-be parents, Mack got straight to the purpose of their visit. ''Jamie has been gone for about three weeks,'' he said in a worried tone. ''He's a level-headed, self-reliant kid, but eleven is way too young for him to be on his own. We're hoping that you can help us locate him. Where did the Dawsons live that summer while Jessie roamed along the dunes, painting her wildflowers?''

''They stayed at a trailer court just back from where I had my shop.'' Mrs. Silverstone gave the little picture a last sad glance and then returned it to Mack. ''It was a dinky, ramshackle place with eight or nine units that overlooked the dunes. None of them in very good repair, I'm afraid, but it was a roof over their heads. 'So what if it leaks?' Jessie said. 'There isn't enough rain to worry about in the summer.' '' She sighed. ''I always thought of it as camping out, but scrimping on the rent was a real necessity in their case. By living thriftily while they were here, Jessie could save the money she earned from her paintings to see them through the following winter.''

''That sounds very sensible,'' Holly said. ''But it's strange we didn't notice a trailer court near Sunset Moods.''

''The place no longer exists. Last winter, mud slides washed one of those trailers right off the bluff and tumbled it down toward the dunes that keep moving farther inland every year. The authorities ordered the rest of the units towed off. Said they were a menace to life and limb.''

Behind her glasses, the sparkle of hope in Holly's eyes dimmed. Another dead end! A few more questions demonstrated that there was nothing else of use that the woman could tell them. They thanked her for her time and returned to the street. Back in the van, Holly turned to Mack with an uncomfortable question: ''Why did you stop me from telling her the truth?''

He kept his gaze fastened on the seat belt he was struggling to adjust. ''Because it made Mrs. Silverstone happy to believe that Jamie was going to acquire a wonderful family. A *whole* family. Just like it tickles Phoebe to think that she has a pair of devoted lovebirds staying at her bed-and-breakfast. What harm does it do to let two nice old ladies hold on to their fairy tales?''

"None, I guess." Holly might have known that he wouldn't have missed the innkeeper's natural assumption that a tender relationship existed between them. "When we first arrived, I tried to convince Phoebe that you and I weren't, uh, involved. But I suspect she prefers to believe otherwise."

Mack gave his one-shouldered shrug. "So let her believe whatever makes her happy. Some people are natural romantics."

His matter-of-fact expression clearly implied that other people were not. Holly felt certain that he included himself among this latter group.

"Mrs. Silverstone might not have been willing to tell us anything if she had suspected we were squabbling over Jamie," she conceded. "Not that what she did have to say was any big help, as it turned out."

"I know. It's like playing one of those frustrating board games." Mack sighed. "One move forward, two steps back."

His discouraged tone bothered Holly. Usually, he was a very upbeat person. It did her heart good a moment later to see his jaw tighten in renewed determination.

"Are you game to go prowling around that old trailer court?" he asked. "Maybe we can scare up a few clues."

"Sure," she said. Her spirits lifted a notch as she used a bright tone to bolster his. "We've been doing great so far. Especially for a pair of amateurs. Why, in just a few days we've made far more progress than Pete Gordon did in almost three weeks.''

''Yeah, but to give the devil his due, your private eye knew nothing of Jamie's good old days.'' Mack cast her a sympathetic look. ''I wish he'd been a better detective, so you could at least have gotten your money's worth. It must have cost a pretty penny to hire him.''

''Boy, did it! A great-aunt left me a little inheritance last year. Otherwise, I never could have swung his fees.'' But she was a blessings counter, and she added, ''At least I'm not reduced to living under a leaky roof like poor Jessie Dawson.''

Now that they knew where to look, the unpaved road curving off behind the craft shop was not hard to spot. Remembering the winter mud slides, Holly proceeded along it very cautiously. A hundred feet from the cliff's edge, striped wooden barricades blocked the way. She swung the van to the left and pulled up at a small roadside park.

Wax myrtle and shore pines sheltered a few picnic tables and barbecue pits. The undergrowth between the trees was wild rhododendrons, with a few fragrant pink blossoms lingering past their season to perfume the salt air. Holly stepped out onto a cushion of pine needles, then reached back for her sweater. After helping Mack drape his denim jacket across his injured shoulder, she strolled beside him to where authoritative KEEP OUT! signs warned trespassers away from the site of the demolished trailer court.

"The brambles have taken over already," she noted in a small, choked voice. "There's nothing left to show that people ever lived here at all."

Hearing the bitter disappointment in her words, Mack knew that until now Holly hadn't been able to make herself believe that no trace of the place still existed. She had been confident they would find something, maybe one forgotten dwelling that a runaway child could use for shelter.

Impulsively wrapping his left arm around her shoulders, he gave her a quick, fortifying hug, which was not much to offer in the way of comfort, Mack thought. If he could have come up with a better method of easing her woes, he'd have done it like a shot. But deep inside, he knew that it was a little boy who would bring the gladness back to her smile, and not some wounded warrior who had never been any good at pretty words.

A frown spiked between his dark brows. "We aren't licked yet," he growled. "Let's give this some deep thought. Say that Jamie did come here, just like we figured. And suppose he found the trailer court gone. What would he do next?"

The point-blank question jerked Holly out of the doldrums, and forced her to battle back against despondency and to cudgel her brain for some logical answers.

"He might decide to stay, regardless," she murmured after a thoughtful pause. "He's a mighty ingenious kid. I know Jamie can build a campfire and cook over it. And there's plenty to eat right here this time of year for someone who'd know where to look for it. Berries by the ton. And other fruit too, and nuts, and clams and oysters out there in the water. I also wouldn't be surprised to find the remnants of an old vegetable garden in that level patch over there beyond that stump."

"Stay here," he said. "I want to have a look at the rest of the terrain."

Skirting the barriers, Mack paced forward to the edge of the bluff. From there he could have done a swan dive three hundred feet straight down into undulating waves of sand. The dunes stretched from the foot of the cliff westward for at least another quarter mile before the surf foamed in to meet the pervasive sand.

He called back over his shoulder, "Can Jamie fish?"

"Of course! What country boy can't?"

Catching the pulse of excitement in his tone, Holly steeled her courage and moved forward to stand beside him. The windswept heights made her blanch with fear, but she forced herself to peer down. "A jetty!" she cried, spying an old narrow pier stretching out into the deep, blue Pacific.

"This must be the place Phoebe mentioned. I'll bet you can catch some dandy bass and sea trout right out there." Mack grinned, recalling his own boyhood exploits with a bamboo pole and a can of wiggly bait. His jubilation mounted as he spotted an overgrown trail. He took a cautious step toward it.

Holly grabbed for his shirttail and pulled him back.

"Mack, you idiot! Your arm's in a cast! What good would it do Jamie if you broke your neck?"

He'd sure been right about where her concerns lay, Mack thought wryly. It wasn't the notion of his breaking his neck that she minded, just the effect a bad accident would have on their quest.

But as much as he hated to admit it, she was right too. It wouldn't help Jamie at all if he hurt himself trying to prove he was Captain Marvel instead of ordinary Captain MacKinnon. One-handed, he couldn't hope to make it safely to the bottom of the precipice, much less climb all the way back up again.

"There's a road," Holly continued. "I saw it when we got out of the van." Still anxious to keep him from attempting anything foolhardy, she led him back to the little roadside park. From there, she pointed to the far side of the picnic tables.

"There," she said, wishing she didn't have to look. "We can get down that way."

Really, she thought, as he agreed to do it her way, it was a travesty to call that path a road. In truth it wasn't much more than a parallel pair of ruts roller-coastering down the craggy side of the bluff. Only one thing in the world could have made her attempt to tackle it in a car—the conviction that if she was too cowardly to do so, Mack was going to try it on foot. And he already had a Purple Heart, she reminded herself sternly. With clusters, no doubt. Not that he even needed medals to prove his valor. One look would tell anyone that this Marine was hero material.

A glimpse of her ashen face moved Mack to protest. ‘‘Holly, that’s a fearsome drop without any guardrails. Are you sure you want to risk your van on a road like that?’’

She swung into the driver’s seat, stretched the shoulder harness across her body, and stared at him in challenge. ‘‘I’m sure. Unless you don’t want to take a chance that I might not get you down safely.’’

‘‘I’d trust you with my life,’’ he answered without hesitation.

‘‘Then hold on!’’

His unexpected pat on the back gave wings to her self-confidence, but a few seconds later, Holly was wishing there was a way the blue-and-silver Aerostar could also have been handed an aerodynamic assist. Its hood tilted perpendicularly. Gears and brakes dragged from the fearful pull of gravity. Tires humped over rocks, slewed across branches, fought their way free from tangles of vegetation.

They had traveled no more than a few yards downhill when her ears caught the rasping snarl of an engine approaching at high speed. It drew even with the park, then faded in the distance down the Coast Highway. The obstreperous racket sounded horrifyingly familiar. Twice in the past week, an identical uproar had split her ears and struck terror into her heart.

But Holly refused to let the brute threat of machinery undermine her assurance this time. A split second’s loss of concentration, she knew, could send them cartwheeling out into space. Mack was depending on her.

So was Jamie. She couldn't let them down. Closing her mind to everything but the jolting road, she kept going.

Before she could even release her taut-held breath, they were down to sea level. Thick with trees and outcroppings of rock, the cliff buffered away noise from the rude world above. A few hundred yards off, the ocean frothed and the surf whispered in a sibilant dialogue. Between ness and water sprawled the dunes, row after row of sandy hills. Some were shallow, with grasses growing in weed-patch abandon at their fringes. Others were deadly deep, and crowned with the bleached skeletons of trees marooned for all time in the suffocating wastes.

Suddenly, a sight even more fantastic than the strangled forest met their eyes. Over the ridge came a dog in harness, leading a well-trained pack of five more pairs of Siberian huskies. Without the least semblance of effort, the animals pulled a man who rode, clasping their reins, upon a rectangular platform mounted on four puffy wheels.

Spotting the couple who stood watching in open-mouthed amazement, the driver called his animals to a halt and then hopped down from the outlandish rig.

"You look surprised," he said with a laugh.

"I'm absolutely flabbergasted!" Holly pushed her long hair back from her eyes, as though making sure he wasn't just in her imagination. "What on earth is a dogsled doing out here?"

"Practicing for a race." Clark Eisner introduced

himself, and then added that if he lived in Alaska, he would be preparing to compete in the Iditarod.

"That's a grueling competition held every March along a 1,168-mile course," he explained. "It recreates a historic relay that took place in 1925, when dogsleds were used to carry lifesaving serum from Anchorage to Nome during a diphtheria epidemic."

"I've heard of the Iditarod, of course," Mack said, and then admitted that he hadn't known the history of that famous big-money run at the top of the world. "Is there actually a race held out here on the dunes too?"

"Sure thing, but it's more for fun than for profit." Clark patted one of his dogs. "We're preparing for the Oregon Dune Mushers' Mail Run. It's a fifty-mile race from North Bend to Florence. We hold it to commemorate the good old days when traffic moved up and down this coast only by sailing ships and stagecoaches."

At his use of the phrase "good old days," Holly and Mack stiffened to attention, because it instantly reminded them of the reason they had come to this isolated beach. At once, Mack skewed the conversation to a topic he hoped might aid in their search for Jamie.

"I suppose you encounter quite a lot of surprised people when you're out practicing," he said lightly.

"Oh, sure. Down by Hauser, dune-buggying is a popular sport, so I avoid that area most of the time." The sledder chuckled. "This far north, the people I meet are mostly either beachcombers or fishermen, and I probably wind up as another tall tale their listeners don't believe, like the ones about the ten-foot salmon that got away.''

''How about children?'' Holly asked.

''On nice days we see a few members of the sand-bucket set,'' Clark allowed. ''Their parents are usually leery of the dogs and I can't say I blame them for that.'' He reached down to scruff the thick, lush fur of one of the gray-and-black Eskimo dogs. ''Each of my huskies weighs pretty close to a hundred pounds, but if there's no adult to hold them back, older kids are sometimes intrepid. There's one kid I've encountered twice who actually comes running out to meet us. He seems lonesome for company, even if it's just the four-footed kind.''

''Sometimes that's the best kind,'' Mack observed. ''Whereabouts was it you ran into this boy?''

The sledder took his time about answering. He looked Mack over very carefully with clear, steady eyes that seemed used to assessing people's character.

''Right in this area, as a matter of fact,'' he replied at last. ''Both times I saw him, he was fishing off that jetty.''

Holly swallowed hard to get her churning hopes under control. Quickly, she removed the enlargement of a photo from her shoulder-strap purse. Her fingers trembled ever so slightly as she extended the picture toward Clark.

''Is this the boy you've seen out here?''

Clark's eyes narrowed as he glanced from the photo

back to her. ''Who is this kid?'' he demanded harshly. ''The long-lost heir to a throne or something?''

Of all the reactions they might have expected, this was the most surprising. ''Of course not,'' Mack exclaimed impatiently. ''He's an eleven-year-old orphan named Jamie Dawson. Jamie ran away from home three weeks ago. Everybody's been worried sick about him.''

''At least you two plus somebody else.''

Holly stared at the man in bewilderment. ''Somebody else? *Who?*''

''Lady, I'm afraid that's your problem.''

Clark flipped down the goggles he had pushed up onto his forehead earlier. With a sharp motion of his gloved hand, he called his dogs to order. Then, resting a booted foot on the platform of his sled, he glanced back over his shoulder for a parting shot:

''Weird coincidences tend to make me suspicious, that's all. Maybe you two are okay. Or maybe the other guy was. All I can tell you is that I ran into him yesterday. He showed me that very same photo—and said there was a big reward out for a kidnapped child.''

Chapter Eight

"Kidnapped!"

Holly felt as though someone had given her a good, hard shove. Her thoughts were reeling. By the time she collected her scattered wits, Clark Eisner and his team of huskies had mushed almost out of sight.

Staring after their fast-receding backs, she was tempted to believe that the dunes sledder had merely been a mirage. But a glimpse of the turmoil on Mack's face put an end to any such fancy.

"Jamie wasn't kidnapped," she protested in bewilderment. "He ran away of his own free will. And he has no family to post a reward for his return. Mack, what's going on?"

Had it been an enemy sniper suddenly opening fire on him, Mack could have handled the situation with levelheaded efficiency. But nothing in his experience had prepared him to field the confusing allegations the other man had just tossed at them.

He didn't know *what* to believe. For a few grim seconds he was swamped with doubts. Had everything Holly told him been a lie? Common sense stifled that moronic notion before it could get out of hand. *He* was the one who had told *her* about Jamie's yearning for the good old days. Who had supplied the directions bringing them here to the Dunes Coast. Who had instigated the search leading to Etta Silverstone. It would be a miracle, Mack told himself, if Jamie's teacher wasn't harboring some serious suspicions about *him!*

Astonishingly, that didn't seem to be the case. Behind her glasses, Holly's eyes looked stunned, but no mistrust lurked in their depths. With beads of perspiration dappling his forehead, Mack dropped his gaze to the photo in her hand.

"Someone fed our friend with the dogsled quite a line," he growled. "It must have sounded reasonably plausible, though. Otherwise, he wouldn't have spooked when you showed him that picture. Maybe he thought that we had done the kidnapping and then misplaced our victim before we could collect the ransom."

Holly remembered the skeptical look on Clark Eisner's face. "That would explain why he took to his heels in such a hurry. He sure didn't wait around to hear our side of the story."

"Earlier, you passed up a chance to look at Jamie's

letters. Maybe you ought to change your mind and read them now.''

She blinked in confusion. Was there something about all this drifting sand that caused people to make outrageous suggestions? ''Why on earth would I want to do that?''

''Just to make sure that I'm not the one telling tall tales.''

''I *am* sure.'' Gravely, steadily, she stared back at him. ''I had a long time to get to know you through your letters, Alexander MacKinnon. No half-baked suspicions of a total stranger are going to make me believe you'd tell lies about Jamie.''

Relieved, Mack ran a sleeve across his damp brow. ''Thanks, Holly. It means a lot to hear that you have that kind of faith in me. But *somebody* is doing his best to muddy the waters, and he didn't want Eisner to talk to us about spotting the boy in that picture here on the beach.'' He scowled at the photo. ''Where did that come from, by the way?''

Holly glanced down at the color print of a freckle-faced youngster. ''It's just an ordinary school photo. A photographer comes around once a year and takes individual shots of all the children as well as group poses of the various classes. Timberline School was scheduled to have our pictures taken in February, but there was a chicken pox epidemic that month and the camera session was postponed until the first week in May.''

''So it's a brand-new picture?''

"Uh-huh. The prints came back just a week or so before Jamie ran away. As soon as I got back from North Carolina, I had this pose of Jamie enlarged and two copies reprinted."

"One for you. . . ."

"And one for Pete Gordon. He needed it to show around places."

"Sounds like he's still doing exactly that."

She shook her head. "That's silly, Mack. I *fired* him!"

"Yup. I heard you."

"Private eyes don't work unless they have a client who's willing to pay them."

"It's easy to tell that you're a schoolteacher," Mack commented. "You have a good, solid grip on logic."

The Marine captain was a man of action, and Holly wondered if he was mocking her attempts to find a rational solution to the problem. To Mack, standing around and trying to reason it out might seem like a wimpy procedure. She was inclined to think he was probably right, but gathering facts and attempting to make sense of them were the only weapons in her arsenal.

Doggedly, she persisted. "I'm not his client any longer, so Pete Gordon wouldn't have any reason to continue the search for Jamie." She bit her lip. "Even if he wanted to do so, how would he know to come here?"

"Maybe he followed us."

The suggestion gave Holly a sinking sensation. The

insidious dunes had swallowed whole thickets and had turned living trees into phantom groves. Now they were bogging *her* down as well.

"Why?" she asked.

"I don't know."

"*How?*"

Though trained to fight when necessary, Mack was no slouch when it came to using his intellect, and his eyes narrowed. "Think back, Holly. What woke you up in the middle of the night on Saturday?"

"The thud of a car door closing. At first I thought that maybe a thief had tried to steal the van. But when I found my glasses and a flashlight, I discovered that it was still there, untouched."

"Are you sure? Suppose someone stopped out there on the road, walked quietly up your driveway, and planted a little gadget somewhere on the van where you'd never notice it?"

Mack's suggestion had the impact on Holly of a verbal hand grenade.

"*Bugged* it, you mean? Like spies do in the movies?"

"Exactly like spies and other shady characters do in real life."

A private investigator would have access to electronic devices for keeping tabs on a subject, she conceded reluctantly. In fact, such things would probably be part of his stock-in-trade. "But he'd have no reason to do that," she protested. "I made it perfectly clear over the phone that I was dispensing with his services."

"So you did. Gordon couldn't have had any doubt that he'd been fired. Particularly after you informed him that you and I intended to search for Jamie ourselves—with some inside information that would help us find him in short order."

"I was exaggerating," Holly said weakly. "He made me mad, calling me 'little lady.'"

"I have a hunch he also decided to call your bluff."

The notion of being tailed all the way from Spruce Ridge to the seashore gave Holly the creeps. She paled as she recalled something that made it seem even more likely that Mack was correct. "Remember my telling you that that big pickup truck that nearly ran us off the road sounded just like the vehicle I heard roaring down the grade from my cabin?"

Was it Gordon playing cat and mouse? Mack wondered. At the time, he'd taken it for granted that the inconsiderate trucker was just a mean, pushy drunk. But Holly's suggestion added a new perspective to the road hog's motives.

"There's more," she confessed morosely. "An hour or so ago, when we were driving down here to the beach, I heard that same snarling motor thunder past on the Coast Highway." She scrunched up her brow in bewilderment. "But that doesn't make sense. If we're right about him following us, why would he go on past?"

Mack had walked over to the van and hunkered down behind it. "Maybe because he'd lost track of us and was trying to pick up the trail again," he suggested.

"Here's a little piece of evidence to bolster my theory." Straightening up, he held out his left hand. In its broad palm rested a small metallic object.

"That thing looks squashed," Holly said blankly. "All flattened out."

"How 'bout that?" Mack grinned. "Anyone would think a ticked-off lady driver might have done something impulsive, like bashing it up against a big ole ugly trash container."

Holly blushed. Ticked-off at *him,* she remembered. And then even more burned at herself for whacking the restaurant's dumpster with such force that she damaged her bumper. But now—"Talk about blessings in disguise!" she cried. "Do you suppose the impact might have made that gizmo's beeper stop beeping?"

Mack looked down at the mangled device. "I'd say you slew this little dragon in a big way. Now all we have to do is figure out why it was put there in the first place." He met her eyes. "Why did Gordon bother to bug your van? What's in it for him that would make him go to all this trouble?"

Holly didn't know the answers to those puzzling questions. "We could ask Krista, his secretary," she suggested.

"Good thinking," Mack said, and then groaned. "I want to stay right here in case Jamie shows up. But for his sake as well as ours, it's vital we learn what Gordon is trying to pull. Let's get to a phone and check up on that shady shamus."

This time Holly didn't object to his nomenclature.

She didn't care what uncomplimentary terms he used to refer to the private detective. But she did protest, as they piled into the van, to his bringing along the squashed electronic device.

"Mack, I wish you'd throw that thing away! It—it's sinister!"

With a firm shake of his head, he tucked the offensive gadget into the glove compartment. "I don't like what it represents, either, but you've already shown it who's boss, remember? And it's possible we might need it for evidence when we confront this joker."

Earlier, Holly had worried about her ability to maneuver the van back up that abysmal track to the top of the bluff. The thought of two cars trying to squeeze past each other on the steep, narrow lane was enough to turn any driver into a devout pedestrian. Fortunately, the road to the jetty was seldom traveled, and no other vehicle was in sight as the Aerostar surged up the precipitous grade.

Emerging into the small roadside park, Holly paused for a minute to catch her breath. "I've been thinking about that man with the dogs," she said. "It's lucky you asked him about people he met while out sledding on the dunes before I sprang the photo on him."

"Knowing for sure that Jamie has been seen in this neighborhood is a real plus." Mack's jaw firmed. "Unfortunately, we have to proceed on the assumption that he gave the same information to the first person who showed him that picture."

Holly resisted the temptation to stop at Sunset Moods

and ask to use Loomis Tugman's phone. The craft-store owner had already made one call for them, and, more important, she felt impelled to safeguard their movements by keeping them as confidential as possible. Having accidentally discovered the bug hidden beneath the van's crumpled bumper gave them a slight edge over Pete Gordon, and if they hoped to turn the tables on the skunk, it was vital to keep him from learning that he was under suspicion.

Not long afterward, as they drove into the village of Glenada, Holly spotted an old-fashioned phone booth outside a convenience store, and she pulled over to it. Mack also got out and headed for the glass enclosure. About to object that the boxy space was too tight a fit for a second person, especially one with his arm in a big, heavy cast, Holly changed her mind. Mack and she were partners, and he had a right to learn what was going on at the same instant she herself received the information.

After squeezing inside, they levered the folding door shut to close out street noises. Holly used her phone card to reverse the charges to her home number. Then she dialed the business office in downtown Eugene. After the fourth ring, her anxious eyes collided with a solemn gray gaze. Even when exchanging a kiss last night, they hadn't been nearly this close, and she found Mack's muscular masculinity extremely disconcerting. *Please, Krista, answer the phone!*

Five, six, seven rings. Where the devil was Gordon's secretary? Mack wanted to scream. Being wedged against this female's soft, slender contours was causing his heartbeat to skyrocket. Gazing down on the pale, silky spill of her hair, he felt a rush of protectiveness, and an impulse to shield and safeguard. And also another emotion. He'd known girls who were more stunning if not more beautiful, and he had dated alluring, sophisticated women on five continents. But Holly Smith was captivating in a deeper, more elemental way than any of those brief companions had been. It was downright unsettling, the way he was reacting to her.

Eight, nine, ten. Holly didn't know how much longer she could maintain her composure. Long before setting eyes on him, she had been more than half in love with Alexander MacKinnon. The yellow ribbons had been a personal plea to heaven to bring him home safely. His letters had shown him to be an honorable, sensitive, and caring man. Since he'd shown up on her doorstep, a few more complimentary terms had been added to her assessment of the man: trustworthy, magnetic, *devastating*.

Eleven, twelve. . . .

The measured rings were interrupted by a breathless response: "Hello! Gordon's Investigations!"

"Krista!" Holly sounded like a drowning swimmer who has just been thrown a life preserver. "I was beginning to think I'd dialed the wrong number. This is Holly Smith, Denise's friend. I consulted your boss about a missing child, remember?"

"Of course I do. But as of yesterday, Mr. Gordon became my ex-boss. I got tired of trying to inhale around those cigars of his, and accepted a new position in a smoke-free building. I just dashed in this afternoon to water the plants because I knew Mr. Gordon planned to be out of town, and I was afraid that poor philodendron would die in this hot weather.''

''Out of town?'' Holly asked lightly. ''Where did he go?''

''Over to the coast, I think. He got a new lead on your case. I heard him tell someone he hopes to wind it up in a hurry.''

Holly caught her breath in shock. ''But didn't he tell you—?'' She felt a sharp nudge from Mack, and saw him shake his head in warning. *Don't share the news that Gordon has been fired with his blabbermouth ex-secretary,* he seemed to be cautioning. ''Where you can contact him?'' she asked instead.

''I can't. But I did get the impression that he intends to pull out all the stops to try and find that little boy.''

''Why the sudden activity?'' Holly hoped she didn't sound as suspicious as she felt.

''Oh, he has his motives,'' Krista replied. ''One of the big philanthropic organizations is funding a new foundation to locate missing children. Word is out that there'll be at least one opening—with a fat annual retainer, of course—for a private investigator with plenty of experience in that line.''

''Do you mean to tell me that he's just using Jamie as the means to an end?''

''You wouldn't *believe* the competition for a plummy job like that. Mr. Gordon's record hasn't been so good lately, and he needs all the successful finds he can rake up if he hopes to snag the spot for himself."

Glancing up, Holly caught the raw anger fulminating across Mack's face. He'd heard Krista's every word and was seething with rage. She gripped his bronzed forearm, attempting to defuse his wrath. She was mad too, infuriated, but blind anger would only eat away like acid at their tempers, and maybe even trip up their plans to thwart the self-serving detective.

Her cool-down stratagem worked. Beneath her calming touch, Mack visibly relaxed.

"Ask what sort of vehicle her ex-boss drives," he murmured a reminder.

"Hey, who's that with you?" Krista asked. "He sounds mighty close."

"Uh, Mack is another interested party in this search for Jamie," Holly explained.

"To me, he sounds like an *interesting* party," commented the unsquelchable Krista. "In answer to your friend's question, Mr. Gordon drives a big, black Dodge Ram pickup, and it's fitted with humongous tires—you know, the kind that lift it twice as high as anything else on the road. I think he has a couple of spotlights on the roof too."

Despite the day's heat, a shiver rippled along Holly's spine. *So we guessed right!* her eyes said as they met Mack's.

This time it was his turn to soothe her. He splayed his left hand across her shoulder, the warm touch of his fingers sending calming tingles all through her.

Both Mack and Holly gulped down deep, steadying breaths of fresh air as they pushed themselves free of the phone booth. Neither was in any hurry to return to the van, where they would once again be thrown together in unsettling proximity. He gestured toward a convenience store and said, "Could you go for a cold drink?"

"Could I! My throat is as dry as one of those dunes we just visited."

Mack paid for the refreshments while Holly carried the two tall paper cups back outside. He was now even more worried about Jamie. Of course, he reminded himself, that was just as true for Holly. She had spent that inheritance from her great-aunt on trying to locate him. Lots of women would have bought themselves a few nice luxuries with the money, but not Holly. She really loved Jamie.

Naturally she loved Jamie, he went on probing at the sore spot. Just like Jamie loved *her*. That fact had come through loud and clear in the boy's letters.

Mack felt like a heel. His caring so much for the youngster had placed him in a real quandary. No way did he intend to back down from his original decision to make Jamie his son. But it seemed mighty unfair to go on planning to take the boy away from Holly.

Mack looked so grim, Holly thought. But of course he would. He had been trained to defend the people and things he loved. His country. The men under his command. And the small boy he'd resolved to take under his wing. Right about now, he must be ready to commit mayhem.

"It isn't right!" she cried. "Pete Gordon is a rank opportunist. For weeks he fooled around, doing practically nothing to try to find Jamie. But now he sees that kid as a ticket to a lucrative new job."

"Well, we aren't going to let him get away with it," Mack said. "That louse has already bugged your van, run us off the road with his truck, and given at least one person the impression that we're kidnappers. I've had enough!"

Even with one arm in a sling, Mack had the air of a gladiator heading out to the arena to tear a lion limb from limb, and Holly was glad he was on her side. Though he wasn't, really. But that didn't matter at the moment, because he certainly was on *Jamie's* side!

"I didn't cave in the bumper until last night," she reminded him. "That means Pete Gordon was able to follow us to the Dunescape Inn on Sunday and Monday. He knows we're staying there, so it'll be simple for him to pick up our trail again."

"That's fine and dandy." Mack deposited his empty cup in a trash container and strode across the sidewalk toward the van. He opened the door, and removed the battered bugging device from the glove compartment.

"Did you say that it's *fine* if that awful man knows where we are?" Holly couldn't believe that she'd heard him correctly.

"Yes, ma'am." Mack bared quite a lot of white, even teeth in an unpleasant grin. "There's an old saying that sums up how challenges are met in the Corps: 'You improvise, you overcome, you adapt.' You and I, Ms. Smith, are about to use that advice in our war against a sleazeball sleuth!''

Chapter Nine

Guiding the van southward on the two-lane Coast Highway, Holly peered cautiously ahead through drifting patches of fog. "I don't dare take my eyes off the road," she said. "Can you tell if he's still back there?"

Outside their windows, the world had a fuzzy, monochrome appearance. It reminded Mack of squinting through an out-of-focus camera screened with a dingy gray filter. But the side mirror reflected the same diffused glow he'd been monitoring for almost an hour.

"Still keeping pace," he reported cheerfully. "Gordon seems to have learned his lesson about crowding us, and he's hanging well back. That string of four or five cars between us and him must seem like pretty good camouflage, but he's forgetting that his truck sits so much taller than the rest of the traffic that his headlights are a dead giveaway."

"Good. I just spotted the city limits sign for Reedsport." Due to the poor visibility, Holly had been driving far below the normal speed limit. Now, as they entered the town, she slowed even more as she said, "Keep your eyes open for a likely looking shopping center."

A few blocks farther on, they spotted a place that seemed ideal. Anchored by a busy supermarket, the string of surrounding stores formed a deep, L-shaped complex. A big coffee shop sat squarely at one end, enticing travelers with promises written in neon.

"Perfect!" Holly breathed. "Now for the hard part."

Apprehensively aware that a black pickup truck would be prowling up and down the same parking lot, she idled past rows of cars.

"Have a look!" Mack nodded toward a vehicle approaching from the opposite direction. It pulled to a halt in front of the restaurant.

Holly could scarcely believe their luck. The van he had spotted was a slightly later model but otherwise almost identical to her own. Hoping that the detective who had been tailing them for the past twenty-odd miles was content to hang back and watch the blip on his screen instead of getting too close, she U-turned around to park next to the other Aerostar.

"California plates," Mack observed.

"Let's hope he's headed home."

They opened their doors to step out on the asphalt just as the second couple emerged from their van. ''What a coincidence!'' Four voices, two of them sincere, spoke at once to comment on the resemblance between the cars.

''How's your gas mileage?'' the young husband asked.

Mack, who hadn't driven anything except a jeep in the last year, had to fumble for an answer: ''Even better than the salesman promised!''

''Brr!'' Holly shivered as the damp, chilly air swirled around her. ''The weatherman on the news last night predicted this would lift by noon. I sure hope he's right.''

''You and me both,'' the other young woman replied. She was taller than Holly, but similar in coloring. Lifting her hand, she patted at long, fair hair frizzing rapidly in the trailing mist. ''Fog looks so romantic when you're cuddled up in front of the fireplace. But I certainly don't like driving in it.''

Lacing his fingers through hers, her husband drew her up on the sidewalk. ''Sorry, honey, but we don't have any choice. Vacation's over, and come fog or sunshine, we have to be home in San Diego by Monday morning. Drive safely,'' he called over his shoulder.

''Have a good trip!'' Holly called back.

But as the other couple vanished into the coffee shop, her smile faded. ''What do you think?'' she asked anxiously.

''Made to order.'' Mack had already hunched down

behind Holly's van. With his left hand he fumbled to remove a small gizmo concealed by her distinctive Oregon license plate. "Let me know pronto if they come out again before I'm through here," he warned. "I'd sure hate to try explaining why I'm prying a bug off our bumper and sticking it behind theirs with a heavy-duty magnet!"

Holly was still more than a little doubtful about Mack's scheme, but she had agreed that it was their one sure way of evading Pete Gordon's surveillance and of searching for Jamie without worrying about the detective's interference. She sent a prayer heavenward that the switch would go smoothly.

The previous day, after learning what Krista's former boss was up to, Mack had devised a plan to fool him into setting out on a wild-goose chase. By phone, he'd managed to locate an electronics supply outlet in Eugene, and after learning that the company stocked bugs identical to the one Holly had accidentally flattened, they made a hasty trip back to that city. The sales expert programmed the new device they purchased, assuring them that it emitted the exact type of transmission as the original gizmo. Upon returning to the seashore, they decided to give the substitute a trial run, and Mack flipped a tiny switch to activate the gadget and then stuck it in place.

"We've got company!" he had said only moments after they'd pulled away from the Dunescape Inn. "Head north. We'll pretend to go visit the sea lion caves I keep hearing about. Maybe we can confuse

Gordon into suspecting that Jamie might be hiding someplace up in that direction.''

''The fact that he's still following us means he doesn't have any idea of where Jamie really is,'' Holly said.

''That's right, and it would be a good idea to *keep* him in the dark too. Are you willing to help me take this turkey for a ride?''

''Sure,'' she agreed. ''How long a ride?''

''The farther the better. By now we've probably lulled him into believing that there was just a temporary short in the electronics gadget he planted under your bumper. So we let him stick close while we take him on a little sight-seeing trip.'' Mack laughed. ''Then tomorrow, we'll pull a bit of abracadabra on him and switch the bug to the back of a moving van bound for Kansas City or someplace. Of course, it would be even better if we could find another vehicle similar to this one for him to follow.''

Their luck had held, and now Mack and Holly were crossing their fingers that the private eye would tail the other Aerostar clear across the state line before discovering his mistake.

''I feel guilty, siccing him on a nice young couple like that,'' Holly lamented when the small transmitter had been securely applied to the other van's bumper.

''They'll be okay,'' Mack promised. ''But Gordon is sure to be furious at us when he finds out he's been hoodwinked. I just hope we've got Jamie and are a long way off by the time that happens.'' He took Holly by the elbow. ''Come on, let's go have a cup of coffee. We'll pick a table where we can watch the driveway and make sure nothing goes wrong.''

The bit of razzle-dazzle worked like magic. Twenty minutes later a Ford Aerostar van with California plates turned south onto 101. Three other cars tailgated it out of the shopping-center driveway. A hundred yards behind, an oversized black pickup truck rumbled along in their wake.

''Whew!'' Holly dropped some small change on the table. ''Until this very minute, I wasn't sure it would work.''

''Me too, but I'm relieved that it did.'' Mack scooped up the check. ''Let's go to that deli next door and collect the makings for a good, hearty lunch. Then we'll go stake out that spot on the dunes where Jamie was last seen.''

Within twenty minutes they were en route north again. By the time they passed the mobile-home park where Etta Silverstone resided, the fog had begun to dissipate.

''Looks like the weatherman was right,'' Mack observed with satisfaction.

Holly swung left onto their turnoff. ''Thank heaven! All morning long I've been dreading the idea of tackling that ghastly steep grade again. I—I really don't think I could have managed it in the fog.''

The tremor in her voice didn't go unnoticed. ''Listen, you've been driving quite a while,'' Mack remarked, a little too casually. ''Why don't we take a break? Get out here in the picnic area to stretch our legs?''

Holly was tempted to grab at his suggestion. It would be pathetically easy to postpone the ugly moment of truth. But she wasn't sure that once she stopped, she could make herself go through with it later.

She shook her head. ''Thanks, but I'd better get it over with while I still can.'' After wiping her palms on her pants, she took a death-grip on the steering wheel, and shifted into low.

The van edged tentatively forward while Holly gulped in a deep, life-sustaining swallow of oxygen. It seemed as reluctant as its driver to challenge the almost-perpendicular descent. Then choice was no longer an issue. Deep ruts clawed at the tires. The bone-rattling plunge commenced.

A gull flew by, screaming. The wild shriek echoed in Holly's ears all the way to the bottom of the bluff. She couldn't be certain that her own terrified cry hadn't merged with the bird's. By the time the up-and-down scenery flattened into a rolling panorama of surf-embroidered dunes, her fingerprints felt permanently grooved into the wheel. She pried her shaking hands loose and slumped forward.

Mack had seen terror like that before, often enough to know how destructive it could be unless its victim managed to get an immediate handle on it. He reached over to switch off the ignition. The motor vibration ceased, but Holly continued to tremble.

''That was a sloppy piece of driving if I ever saw

one!'' Mack's old drill instructor would have admired his steely, give-no-quarter tone.

Holly's head jerked up. ''What!''

''You missed that gull by a good three inches.'' Mack shook his head in disgust. ''Shape up, Ms. Smith. It took you only one try to annihilate an expensive chunk of microcircuitry and scare the devil out of an innocent trash dumpster. What's the matter—losing your touch?''

Holly started to laugh. There was a touch of hysteria in the sound, but a lacing of chagrinned humor as well.

''No wonder the Marine Corps intends to promote you,'' she said. ''Any troops come down with battle fatigue, they send you out to bark at them, right?''

''Wrong. DI's bark. People like me take the responsibility if anything goes wrong. Feeling better now?''

Holly postponed answering while she blotted her wet brow. ''I'm fine,'' she then said. ''Peachy. Can't you tell?''

She pushed her way out of the van and held on to the door until her knees stopped buckling. By then she'd run out of bravado. ''Oh, Mack,'' she confessed, ''I'm such a terrible coward. I'd give anything to be brave. But I'm afraid that. . . .''

''Afraid that what?''

''Afraid that the third time will be the jinx.'' Holly grabbed a deep breath to stifle a moan. ''That I won't be spared the next time a catastrophe hits. That the next time, they'll write my obituary.'' She stared at the ground. "I've tried to psych myself into being more courageous, but it doesn't work. Things you'd laugh at scare me witless. Not everyone's a hero like you, Mack."

"Hold on, Holly. You've got the wrong idea of what heroism is all about." Mack had let her get it out of her system, and now he was determined to have his say. "The bravest men I know are cautious, peace-loving guys. They'd walk miles out of their way to avoid a fight unless it's forced upon them."

"Like going to war over there in the Gulf?" She remembered a phrase he'd used a couple of times. "Is that what you'd call 'above and beyond the call of duty'?"

"Nope, just duty pure and simple. But just because you do it doesn't mean you aren't scared stiff at the same time."

"But it was your men you were mostly afraid for, right? You were worried that something would happen to them?"

She seemed to be having trouble accepting the simple truth of what he was trying to get across to her.

"Quit making me out to be something I'm not," Mack ordered. "I was afraid for my men, yes. I was also afraid of getting my head blown off. Everyone has fears—everyone with a lick of sense, that is. Ask anybody who was up there on that line. They'll tell you that courage is something you keep in reserve. You don't even know you have it until you really need it."

"Then it comes to your rescue and sees you through? I never thought about that."

"Look at it this way," he said. "You were sweating buckets coming down that road up there, right? But if you were *really* a coward, you never would have driven down the face of that cliff. Not a *second* time. Not when you already knew what a terrifying experience it was. And that there aren't any guardrails. And no fence to stop you from getting killed if the bank gave way. But you did it anyway, didn't you?"

"Yes," Holly answered, "but only because you couldn't, not with your arm in a sling. And it was important to get back down here. We have to find Jamie."

"Ms. Smith," Mack said, "you just described the actions of a hero."

Giving her no shot at a rebuttal, he turned and led the way across the dunes. Fine, granular sand sucked at their shoes, making progress slow. It didn't matter. Both of them had plenty to think about and no place else to go.

The warped planks of the jetty felt damp and gritty underfoot. Holly wondered if sand particles were trapped in the clammy tendrils of morning fog. Razor-sharp barnacles encrusted the mooring posts. The surf babbled.

"That sounds sort of international, don't you think?" she asked.

Mack cocked an ear to listen, and then nodded.

''Definitely English as a second language. At root, it's something exotic—Polynesian, Melanesian. . . .''

She laughed as she straightened up to stare across the wide blue Pacific. ''I'll bet you know what a lot of languages sound like. You've been out there, haven't you?''

''Everywhere,'' he said with a laugh. ''Well, you know what they say: 'Join the Navy and see the world.' Without leathernecks to establish the beachheads, why would they go?''

He had wanted to keep her amused, but, too soon, her lips resumed their serious set. ''What happened?'' he pushed. ''Those other times that made you talk about obituaries?''

A wave crested, foamed ashore, and receded. As a rule, so as not to tempt fate, Holly kept recollections of those occasions when she'd nearly died buried deep. But Mack claimed she possessed heroic qualities that offset her chickenheartedness. Suddenly she needed to tell him that she hadn't always been scared of her own shadow.

''When I was fourteen, I came down with rheumatic fever,'' she said. ''All my hair fell out, and for months and months and months I couldn't even get out of bed to walk around the house. And my eyes were damaged, so I wasn't allowed to try to study. I missed a year of school.''

She remembered how that had hurt, not being able to graduate with friends who'd been her classmates since kindergarten.

"But you got better." Mack fingered a strand of her long blond hair, as if to say that it had certainly grown in again, prettier than ever.

"Yes," Holly agreed. "A little at a time. Thanks to my brother, who tutored me and recorded hundreds of books onto tape so I wouldn't miss reading so much. And to my mom, who quit a job she loved in order to stay home with me twenty-four hours a day. And to my dad, who worked hard all day, then came home to read to me for hours every night." She smiled at the memory. "Sometimes, if he was behind on a job, he'd read from the blueprints. You'd be surprised what I could tell you about building a house."

Mack was beginning to think that nothing about Holly Smith could surprise him. She was a remarkable woman.

Holly shrugged, and again her smile faded. "After two years of college at home in Asheville, I decided to finish my degree at a university in Florida where they have a wonderful teachers' program."

"You didn't flunk out?" Mack asked in mock horror.

"After all of Gary's tutoring? Perish the thought! But there was a train wreck on the way down to Tallahassee, and the car I was riding in jumped the tracks. Some of the other passengers and I were pinned under the wreckage for an awfully long time."

It was hardly surprising that she was spooked about the third time being unlucky, Mack thought. She'd already had two close brushes with death. "It's a wonder you don't have as many scars as I do," he said.

"Oh, there are a few. I spent the next seven months on crutches," Holly confided. "Once again my parents rallied round and saw me through the dark days. They're absolutely wonderful."

"Naturally. That explains why you left North Carolina and moved to Oregon."

"Of course it does," she agreed seriously. "It was long past time I got on with my life and let the people I love pursue their own interests again instead of just tending to me. Until I was twenty-five, my family was my safety net. They were always there when I needed them. For a change, I wanted someplace that needed *me*. Spruce Ridge fit the bill. It was a tiny mountain community in desperate need of a fifth-grade teacher."

"What happened to their old one?"

"I told you about the woman who owns my cabin. She's doing a hitch with the Peace Corps in Africa."

The woman who's due back next month, Mack recalled. He hadn't realized that when she returned, Holly would be out of a job as well as in need of a new place to live.

"It was your idea for the kids to write those letters to the Gulf," Mack said. "They meant a lot, but I never thanked you." He figured that she was probably sorry now she had ever heard of Operation Desert Storm, or had inspired a letter that began *Dear Marine*. It was through that connection that he'd come to know and love Jamie. Thanks to an act of kindness she had initiated, he now planned to take the boy with him to his new post.

"You never told me why you decided to adopt Jamie," he went on when she didn't answer. "Was that part of needing to be needed too?"

"No." Holly looked as if he'd insulted her. "I want to adopt Jamie because I love him. He needs *someone*, certainly, and he's very fond of me. I think I'll make a good parent and I *know* he'll make a good son."

There was nothing Mack could say to that. He turned away from her, trying to think of a way to defuse this subject that seemed ready to explode in their faces. "I wonder if Eisner brings his dogs out for a run every day."

Holly snatched at this neutral subject with relief. "Pretty often, wouldn't you think? Just in the past few days he's met us and Pete Gordon. And encountered Jamie at least twice in the past. But since he considers us such suspicious characters, I hope he practices somewhere else today. Are you ready for lunch?"

Walking over to get the food from the van, she tried to brush aside the insinuations bristling in Mack's questions. That darned guy seemed to be under the impression she wanted to use Jamie as a crutch, she thought resentfully. That was about as flattering as an assumption that she only wanted the child as an income-tax deduction!

Dejection flowed over her. Strife between them was inevitable, she realized. Mack had come to Spruce Ridge with hopeful plans too. He'd been looking forward to taking on the role of father to a little boy. They couldn't be blamed for resenting each other, not when each intended to try to scuttle the other's ambitions!

Lunch consisted of salami and cheese on crusty rolls, a piquant pasta salad, and cans of soda. By the time they sat down to eat, both had lost their appetites. Leaning against a dune with her back to the sea, Holly nibbled. Mack looked the other way, chewing morosely, not even tasting what he ate. For the past few days they had managed to cooperate in spite of their rivalry. Now, the wedge between them made even a pretense of harmony difficult to maintain.

It was wonderful that Mack had come home safely from the war, Holly assured herself. The answer to a prayer, in fact. But why couldn't he have minded his own business and stayed where he belonged?

Mack wished the stubborn, half-pint schoolteacher the very best. Whatever she did and wherever she went after this wrangle between them was resolved, he hoped she would be happy, healthy, and successful. *Good luck*, he thought, mentally urging her return to the East Coast. With a continent between them, maybe they could manage a peaceful coexistence.

It was easier to look anywhere else than at Mack, with his short-cropped haircut and the pugnacious bump in the middle of his nose. Holly took a swallow of pop and stared up at the high, craggy bluff. A vivid patch of blue caught her eye. Funny, she thought. Blue in the sky, yes. On the sea, of course. But it seemed unnatural on the side of the cliff.

"Mack," she said, breaking the silence in spite of her disinclination to say anything more to him, "remember Mrs. Silverstone mentioning that a trailer slid off its foundations during last winter's storm?"

"Uh-huh," he replied without much interest. "The health department had them all towed away."

Brushing sand off the seat of her pants, Holly stood up and said, "The *other* ones were towed away, the ones that were left. But I'll bet nobody bothered to winch up the old trailer that got washed down the back side of the hill."

"Say, I'll bet you're right." Mack got up too. "It was probably a case of 'out of sight, out of mind.' " He followed her pointing finger to a patch of royal blue fifty yards above their heads. "Wish we had a pair of binoculars. All those bushes and scrubby little trees could be hiding almost anything."

Holly spotted an overgrown trail winding downhill, and felt a pang of remorse. "If I hadn't talked you out of exploring that old footpath the other day, you'd have probably stumbled across it then."

"Stumbled is right. I'd have broken my neck, trying a steep descent like that," Mack admitted. "An *ascent*, now. . . ."

A familiar flicker of trepidation clutched at Holly's heart. There was something different about *this* jab of fear, however. Instead of worrying about her own skin, as usual, it was another person's safety that caused her deep concern.

"Sure, climbing up is different," she agreed, in a

no-big-deal voice. "Let me clamber up and see what I can find. You can stay down here, and point me to the right spot in case I lose sight of it."

"Not on your life," Mack growled, thoroughly vexed. "*I'll* do the climbing."

"How?" Deliberately, Holly stared at the sling binding his right arm.

"I'll *manage*!"

"Under ordinary circumstances, I doubt you'd have a bit of trouble. But you can't handle this by yourself. One of the main differences between us, Mack, is that I learned a long time ago how to accept support from other people, but you just assume you can carry the whole world by yourself. Believe it or not, there are times when everybody needs someone to lean on."

He stood silent a moment, digesting the justice of this accusation. Then, with difficulty, he swallowed his pride. "Want to go together?" he suggested. "Maybe we could lean on each other."

"Sure. Why didn't I think of that?" Holly felt a vast surge of relief. "One last venture won't hurt us, I suppose."

"Us? No way." Mack looked over and raised an eyebrow. "All for one?"

"And one for all," she completed that swashbuckling quotation from *The Three Musketeers*. "Let's go before I lose my nerve. I told you what a rabbit I am."

"I already proved to you that you aren't. If I ever hear you question your courage again, I'll clobber you. Get going," he ordered. "And watch out for snakes!"

"You *would* have to bring up a thing like that!" Nevertheless, Holly moved steadily forward on his right flank.

Mack had known a lot of women in his life—tall, short, wildcat, saccharine-sweet, clinging vines, and take-chargers. But none who had offered him straightforward assistance while expecting the same uncomplicated brand of aid in return. Holly was a true partner, he thought as he levered her up over a boulder after she'd yanked him away from the edge of disaster.

Never, Holly realized in complete exhilaration, had she experienced this sort of camaraderie. Always, before, she had done the leaning. Now, interdependence formed a circle of trust. A tall Marine was depending on her stamina and quick-wittedness for survival. And she needed his help in avoiding some dire pitfalls. They were two key players on the same team.

When the patch of blue they'd spotted from below proved to be only an ancient shred of tarp, Holly was nearly knocked for a loop.

"It's nothing!" she cried, kicking at the useless thing. "Nothing!"

"Lose a few, win a few," Mack said. "Take a look to the left."

Built of wood so weatherworn as to be totally colorless, a shanty leaned drunkenly on an outcrop of rock. It had never been a trailer, Holly knew as she edged toward the tumbledown dwelling. A fisherman's shack, perhaps, once upon a time. Or possibly a habitat for hikers in the very dim past.

They eased across to it and knocked at the splintery, lopsided door. They called out. When no answer came, they ducked low to enter. Inside they stared around at the cramped abode. They saw a cracked plastic window and a jumble of possessions strewn across a mildewed cabinet.

Joyfully, they caught their breath at the sight of a watercolor propped against peeling linoleum. The painting of a wildflower was signed by Jessie Dawson.

Chapter Ten

They waited. Tamping down his eager anticipation, Mack prowled restlessly around the shanty. The time for meeting Jamie face-to-face had almost arrived. Finally.

As he paced back and forth, he discovered new facets of the youngster's personality. With approval, he noted the shipshape way the sleeping bag had been laid out in one corner. Both of them were nature lovers, he was delighted to see. The collection of seashells on the windowsill reminded him of one of his own youthful enthusiasms. Color-streaked agates adorned the sagging countertop. No mean beachcomber himself, Mack remembered similar summer finds, gleaned at low tide from surf-washed scatters of gravel.

A gnarled chunk of driftwood appeared to be a special treasure. Almost as worn, clearly even more treasured, a stack of letters peeked out from beneath the folded flannel shirt that served the boy as a pillow. The return address on the envelopes was an FPO number Mack knew all too well. Seeing them, he forced down a lump of emotion. Jamie might have claimed that he no longer loved his Marine pen pal, but Mack knew better. The bond between them had been forged in ink, but it was as strong and unbreakable as steel. What a joyous lifetime they had ahead of them!

Jamie was a real little nester, Holly thought with pride. Cobwebs festooned the corners of the derelict hut, but he had used moss to keep the wind from whistling through the cracks in the wall. And while the place probably leaked like a sieve through those gaps in the shingles, thc boy's scant supply of food had been wrapped in plastic to keep out the insects.

Propped up next to Jessie's painting was the hilarious birthday card that Holly had given Jamie last April. The fishing gear she'd presented him on the same occasion stood over in the corner. He had treasured it from the start, she remembered. But she felt sure that the gift had turned out to be far more useful than she had ever expected. For the last few weeks, that rod and reel had undoubtedly helped keep the pangs of hunger at bay.

Though he'd managed well, this lonesome existence must have included many trials and tribulations. Holly recalled the barbecue pits in that roadside park on the crest of the bluff. Jamie could have hauled his fish up there to cook over the grill. That way, he'd be far less likely to call attention to his presence than by building a campfire on the sand. But what had he done for fresh water?

Staying warm must have been a problem too, she fretted. Once the sun went down, the ocean breeze could be chilly and damp, especially when the fog rolled in.

At the window, Holly fingered a blue-and-silver mussel shell as she stared through the cracked, yellowing plastic. Down on the dunes, a team of dogs streaked past the jetty. The huskies towed a man on a wheeled sled. She scarcely noticed Clark Eisner, however. It was the mist drifting shoreward across the cobalt blue water that riveted her attention.

"Mack, we have to get out of here!" she cried. "The fog is starting to come in already!"

Striding across the room, he peered in consternation at the whitening scene. "You're right, we can't stay," he agreed, resigned to leaving at once. "Tackling the face of that cliff was tricky enough in decent weather."

Disappointment was evident in every word of his decision. With all her heart, Holly wished that things could have turned out differently for Mack. He had looked forward to meeting Jamie so much, and now that man-to-man encounter would have to be postponed.

"Jamie knows the van," she assured him optimistically. "You'll see, the instant he spots it, he'll come scampering down. We'll wait for him, right there on the dunes.''

For now, though, it was vital that they get down off this steep hill in a hurry. Even with one arm in a cast, Mack was far from helpless. Still, Holly couldn't help worrying about him. This whole week had surely been a terrible strain for a man just out of the hospital. She wished there were something she could do to make it all easier for him.

The day had been warm and sunny when they'd started their upward climb, and it hadn't occurred to either of them to bring along a garment to ward off the chill. As they pushed their way back outside through the warped door, Holly shivered in her sleeveless cotton blouse.

Seeing the tremor, Mack hoped it was caused by the sharp breeze and not panic. Earlier, she'd talked almost fatalistically about the third time being unlucky, and maybe she was worried about falling. He had no intention of letting anything happen to her, but he wasn't sure that she could steel herself to tackle that formidable descent.

''I'll go first,'' he said quickly.

Holly's pale hair swung in an arc as she shook her head sharply. ''Mack, you're able to hold on with only one hand, remember? Let me lead. You'll be fine, of course, but if there *should* be a slip, I can reach up and steady you.''

''And lose your own footing? Nothing doing!''

He sounded adamant, Holly thought. What a stubborn guy! "Together, then," she offered a compromise. "And side by side."

Mack nodded, but in a crunch, he would insist on safeguarding her to the best of his ability. "Okay," he growled. "Get over here to my left. Turn around and face the cliff. We'll crawl down backward."

"Like surmounting an obstacle course in boot camp?"

He grinned at her in reluctant admiration. "You've got it. Let's go. And remember, there's no sergeant down there to catch us if we fall off this thing."

They edged down, one treacherous toehold at a time. The descent seemed interminable. And terrifying. Brambles ripped at their clothing. Nettles stung. Deceptively solid in appearance, rocks rolled loose beneath their grasp and crashed down the precipice with spark-striking thuds. Holly tried not to think of something similar happening to Mack and her.

By the time they reached bottom, she was shaking from cold and exhaustion. The experience had been utterly devastating. Whatever possessed people to go climbing up and down mountains? Still, she felt a thrill of pride in her own relatively tiny achievement as she peered back to where she had been.

Turning away from the bluff, she hurried across to the van. Quickly, she retrieved her sweater and the jacket Mack had worn earlier. "Brr! I wish we had brought along a thermos of coffee!"

"Me too." Mack grimaced at the gritty scum floating on the dregs of his soda pop. Grains of the ever-moving sand had whipped across the drink since he'd set it down. "Did we buy a six-pack of this stuff? My throat could do with some lubrication. Right now it's too parched to get out the words I need to say."

Was he going to make a speech? Holly wondered. She unlooped another can from the plastic-ringed holder for him. "There you go. What was it you wanted to tell me?"

"*Ask,* not tell. There's a difference." Mack wished he could lighten this exchange with a smile, but his features felt starched in place with anxiety. He gave her a stark, straightforward look, and let the question stand on its own. "I was wondering what you'd think about getting married."

Stunned, Holly gaped at him. "You and me?"

"Holly Smith and Alexander MacKinnon," he said, eliminating any possibility of her misunderstanding. "Holly MacKinnon sounds sort of nice, don't you think? Of course, you could keep your own name if you'd rather do that."

No, she wouldn't rather do that. Holly MacKinnon sounded sensational.

Joy shimmered through her as she experimented under her breath with the lovely combination of syllables. How incredible that they should be discussing marriage after the hard feelings that had kept them spitting at each other all afternoon. But now there was no trace of that old enmity in his tone.

Her own antagonism, too, had totally disappeared. While scaling the bluff and then making their way down again, she had felt such kinship with this man, such an intimate linking of their thoughts and hearts that becoming his life partner seemed almost inevitable. How wonderful that the same feelings had mellowed him also!

They would make an incredible match, she thought. Weathering life's rough spots hand in hand. Not that she expected all that many rough spots, because marriage would eliminate their main bone of contention. So long as there was plenty of love. . . .

Holly came down off her rose-colored cloud with a jolt. The man who had just proposed to her hadn't *said* anything about love. Come to think of it, he hadn't even mentioned companionship!

"It might be better to get a few more-important points settled before we start worrying about details like names," she murmured, wary suddenly. "Why do you want to marry me?"

Mack had been raised by stern Presbyterian parents, and his upbringing had included fewer lessons in tact than in telling the unvarnished truth. In the Marine Corps, the slightest deviation from reality could lead to casualties. His whole life had been a training ground for plain speaking.

He wished that she hadn't stressed covering the important points first. He would much rather have told her how much he'd come to enjoy the give-and-take between them, and how drawn he was to her generous and caring nature, and how much he admired that inner courage she had been so quick to deny earlier. He would prefer now to guide her hand to his heart while he told her of the way her soft, lovely womanliness excited his affections. But if she was anxious to deal with the mundane matters first, then that was okay with him. Sentiment could wait.

"It would solve everything," Mack answered. "You don't have a job, and in another month you'll be looking for a place to live. At thirty-two, it's time I was married. There are also career benefits for married officers in the Corps. And Jamie needs parents. He loves us both and we both love him. What could be more sensible than providing him with a mother *and* a father?"

The bald facts hit Holly like icy slaps. "I see," she said. "You're talking about a marriage of convenience."

"Well, sure," Mack said edgily. "Making our partnership permanent *would* be convenient." This wasn't turning out at all the way he'd hoped it would. He had looked for a joyous acceptance of his proposal, not a third degree. "But I certainly wouldn't say that was the most—"

A terrible suspicion had begun to dawn on Holly, and she said, "Why did you wait until now? Why didn't you ask me to marry you three hours ago?"

"Lots of reasons, Holly. Three hours ago we were still arguing, for one thing. We hadn't climbed that cliff together." He still marveled at what a fantastic experience it had been to have her at his side every rugged inch of the way. "We hadn't—"

"We hadn't learned for sure that Jamie was here," she cut in sharply. "But now we know, don't we? Now we've found him. Now he'll need to decide which of us he prefers to live with. And now you're concerned that he won't choose you."

Mack shook his head, longing with all his heart to refute these accusations that he knew to be completely untrue. But how could he tell her that she had it all backward? Seeing those well-thumbed letters under the boy's makeshift pillow had made him realize just how much Jamie really did love him. The boy wouldn't choose to live with his teacher, no matter how devoted he was to her, not if he were given the alternative of having Mack for his father.

It was back there in the cabin that a way to solve the dilemma had occurred to the Mack. If Jamie chose him, it would break Holly's heart. But if she accepted his proposal, there would never be any need to ask Jamie whom he wanted to live with. They could offer him a package deal—two good parents. She need never know she hadn't come first in the boy's affections.

"That's not true, Holly," he told her. "I don't know how to convince you, but that isn't the reason I asked you to marry me." Mack felt as though he were trapped between a rock and a hard spot. "Don't you see, it isn't fair to ask an eleven-year-old kid to make the kind of decision that can affect his whole life. It would be so much better if we just. . . ."

"Merged?"

"United! Became a family!"

"Thank you very much," Holly said in a stiff, hurt tone. "But the answer is *no*. I wouldn't want to marry anyone who just wanted me around as a live-in mother."

"I want a whole lot more than that. I want a wife who'll stand by me and our kids, come hell or high water!"

"That's exactly the sort of wife I intend to be—for the man who loves me." Holly's eyes were glistening with tears. "But since I haven't met him yet, I consider this discussion pointless."

Mack stared at her in astonishment. How could she stand there and accuse him of not loving her? How could she assume he would ever ask any other woman to share his life?

It occurred to him then that she hadn't given him time to get to the sweet and tender elements of his proposal. He'd jumped to the conclusion that, to her, "important" details meant practical considerations. Now, much too late, he realized that Holly had been waiting to hear him tell how much he cherished her, wanted her, needed her. And, especially, loved her.

She would never believe him, he thought gloomily. Not now. Not when she had practically coached him and he still hadn't said the words. But he had to try to convince her.

"Ms. Smith! Is that *you?*"

With one astonished motion, the wrangling couple down on the dunes spun to stare up at the side of the bluff. They had been so intent on their discussion that neither of them had been aware of the fog drifting past the line of breakers to obscure the landscape with damp, clinging tendrils. But now the view of both water and bluff was screened by an opaque curtain and only patches were visible.

"There!" With tremendous relief, Holly pointed to a splotch of red up on the cliff. "Jamie!" she called. "Jamie, I'm here!"

"Who's that with you?" the boy's piping voice demanded.

Mack answered for himself: "Do you want my name, rank, and serial number, or will just plain Mack do?"

"Mack!"

The tremendous joy in that cry went straight to Mack's heart. He'd been right, he thought. This was *his* boy, no doubt about it. But how was he going to keep Holly from getting hurt?

The moment of truth was galloping toward them at breakneck speed, Holly thought in desperation. That emotional look on Mack's face when he heard the boy call his name was convincing testimony to how much he loved Jamie.

How in the world was she going to keep this wonderful, well-meaning man from being hurt? Up there in that old shanty, she had seen indisputable evidence to prove that Jamie loved her dearly. As soon as she spotted that birthday card propped up next to Jessie's watercolor, she had known there was no possibility that the boy would choose anyone else but her to be his parent. No matter how much Mack's letters had meant to him.

Mack himself had come up with the perfect solution, she thought mournfully. She was already wild about the man. If he hadn't made it embarrassingly clear that he regarded their marriage as little more than a business deal, her saying yes would have been the ideal answer to their problem.

She would have had the husband she adored. Jamie would have had two devoted parents. And Mack would never have needed to know he had placed second in the boy's affections.

But it wasn't going to work. With her own parents' strong, devoted marriage as a shining example, Holly knew that she could never settle for marrying a man who wasn't at least sincerely fond of her.

"I'm coming down!" the boy shouted from up on the bluff. "Wait right there for me, you guys!"

"We will! Jamie, please be careful!" Holly clasped her hands anxiously as she heard the ominous rattle of scree rolling down the cliff.

"Kids that age are part mountain goat," Mack sought to reassure her, trying not to reveal his own nervousness.

Fortunately, in the last two weeks, Jamie had had so much practice scrambling up and down the trail to the beach that even in the fog he managed the descent with very little trouble. Within minutes the youngster in the red shirt and ragged blue jeans hopped nimbly down the last foot or two of slope and then barreled across the dunes. His outstretched arms wrapped Holly and Mack in one vast jubilant hug that showed how overjoyed he was to see them.

"You came!" he cried rapturously. "You came all this way to get me! But how did you find out where I was?"

"Mack guessed where to look from the letters you wrote him," Holly said, giving credit where it was due. "The last batch of mail finally caught up with him in the hospital."

Mack started to protest that it had been a joint venture all the way. That he couldn't have done it without Holly. But Jamie had reacted in shock to the word "hospital" and was staring up with round, fearful eyes at Mack's plaster cast.

Stooping down to the boy's level, Mack gave him an awkward, one-armed hug. "Nothing to worry about, son," he said gently. "As I guess you can see, a little problem cropped up to keep me from answering a few of those great letters you sent me. But I'm okay! Got it? Now that we've found you, there's nothing more to worry about."

"Oh, yes there is," Holly contradicted him in a tight, scared tone.

Mack straightened up in a hurry, swinging around to follow her stricken gaze. A huge pickup truck had swooped out of the fog like some malevolent black vulture and was thundering downhill toward them at breakneck speed.

Chapter Eleven

The threesome froze for a dumbfounded moment, gaping in horror at the massive truck bearing down on them. Along the rutted track it roared, muscling through the fog with the fearsome power and noise of a speeding locomotive.

Mack was the first to recover. "Jump for the van!" He half-scooped, half-shoved Jamie toward relative safety and then tumbled after Holly as she wrenched open the driver's door and catapulted into her seat. Keys dangled from the ignition, left there hours ago when Mack had turned it off. She snapped the motor to life, hardly remembering that attack of nerves. She flicked on headlights and jammed her foot down on the accelerator.

"Easy, easy," Mack warned as horsepower surged

and the Aerostar leaped forward. ''Don't skid off the pavement. We'll wind up spinning our wheels in the sand.''

And being fair game for that vindictive predator! It was hard not to run blindly away with something the size of the Dodge Ram bearing down on them. The other driver's aggressively blasting horn seemed to signal his intentions of running them into the dunes—at least!

''Oh, no!'' Holly moaned. ''We're literally trapped between the devil and the deep blue sea. That man's a lunatic!''

Twin spotlights speared through the fog, pinning the van in their merciless glare. Then the road dipped and the Aerostar broke free temporarily. Down, up, down it bobbed, fleeing the pursuer whose massive tires gnashed through the grit as though taking giant bites out of the pavement.

''Hey, I've seen that truck before,'' Jamie babbled excitedly. ''A big guy with a cigar drove it down here the other day. He acted like he owned the whole beach!''

''Did he get a look at you?'' Mack asked.

''Nope. I'd been gonna talk to the dog man. Then this guy showed up. He sounded loud, and mean. I ducked down behind a big rock and kept still till both of them left.''

''Smartest thing you could have done.'' Mack ruffled the boy's shaggy hair, then flipped a quick glance at Holly. *All right?* his silent gaze inquired.

She nodded, glad to have him there beside her. But how she wished that they were all somewhere else. Anywhere other than here, fleeing into the unknown through a weird, floating landscape.

The fog billowed and tumbled, drifting from dunetop to dunetop while leaving the dipping valleys clear in between. Behind the van, the truck's high beams pierced mercilessly through the least opaque spaces. However, the stabbing amber rays seemed almost to bounce off the thickest patches of fog. Holly lowered her own headlights and found less distortion with the softer glow.

Even so, she was growing increasingly worried. "I can't outrun him much longer," she murmured, wishing Jamie didn't have to hear. "He's just sitting back there playing cat and mouse, or he'd have overtaken us long ago. With visibility practically zilch, I can't even see where I'm going. For all I know, this road could wind up splashing us all in the ocean."

"No, it doesn't go anywhere near the water," Jamie surprised her by saying. "See that bunch of ghost trees up there? The road loops around behind them, then heads back to where we started from."

The van's headlights probed through twisted tangles of deadwood. "Ghost trees is a good name for them," Holly agreed, shivering at the eerie sight.

"Must be one of those groves Phoebe was telling us about," Mack said. He remembered her remarks about small forests being swallowed whole by the encroaching dunes.

Stripped of their bark and leaves, the sapless tree trunks resembled ashen totem poles grotesquely carved by the wind. They were just a natural phenomenon, Holly told herself sternly, and the poor, marooned things might just help them escape the vindictive detective.

She kept her foot firmly on the gas pedal until they had crested another of the knolls. Then, while the downward slope hid them briefly from their pursuer, she suddenly decelerated as she glimpsed the pavement begin to curve. Next, she snapped off the van's lights.

"Hold your breath," she warned. "Without the red glow of our taillights to follow in the fog, he might keep going straight just long enough to bog down in the sand."

"Way to *go,* Ms. Smith!" Jamie yelled in admiration when it happened exactly as she'd hoped. The blue-and-silver van clung to the pavement's narrow curve while the arrogant behemoth behind them roared ahead into the side of a dune.

"Way to *go,* Ms. Smith!" Mack echoed the boy's praises. A big grin spread over his face as his ears picked up the *zzzZZZzzz-zzzZZZzzz* of futilely spinning tires.

Holly wiped her damp palms against her slacks. Then, as the dreadful tension of the last few minutes started to ebb, she took the wheel again in a loose grip.

"Couldn't have done it without your tip about the curve," she told Jamie. Her eyes lifted to meet Mack's. In them was a message of thanks for his earlier encouragement in insisting that she wasn't the coward she had always believed herself to be. "Or without your moral support."

"Another joint venture successfully completed!" Mack declared in satisfaction. "Come on, let's get out of here and call the cops!"

June 24, 1991

Captain A. R. MacKinnon
c/o U.S. Naval Hospital
Bremerton, WA 98310

Dear Mack,

How is your arm? Are the doctors going to take the cast off it pretty soon like you hoped? I was sure disappointed when you had to head out for the hospital almost as soon as I got to meet you. But Ms. Smith told me you promised the doctor you'd report back right away if he let you out of bed to come look for me. She says honerable men always keep their promises, so I guess you had to go.

I'm sure glad the police took that Pete Gordon guy off to jail. It was in the newspaper about the judge taking his lisense away from him and not letting him be a detective any more. I bet they make him ride the bus for a long time too. He sure was a mean driver!

Ms. Smith got permishion for me to stay with her for now. But she says you will help decide my future. Can we do that real soon? Ms. Hickum is coming back from Africa pretty quick and then we will have to move.

Mack, I am sorry for what I said before about not loving you. That was when I thought I was a jinx. Now Ms. Smith says I am not and so I feel okay about saying I love people again.

See you soon, I HOPE.

Love,
Jamie D.

June 27, 1991

Jamie Dawson
c/o Ms. Holly Smith
Timberline Road
Spruce Ridge, Oregon

Dear Jamie,

Thanks for your letter. One of the nurses is writing this for me. My right hand still needs a little more therapy to do things like holding on to a pen. But the cast is off and I'm feeling good.

Ms. Smith is right about my helping to decide your future. I think I know how we can make it a real happy one. So be cool, sit tight, and I'll be there to see you as soon as I can.

Love,
Mack

Day in and day out, the logging trucks rumbled up and down the side of Brother-in-Law Mountain. In the past, Holly hadn't paid much attention to the big rigs. For the past three weeks, however, she had never been able to hear one of them approach without looking up and remembering that hot June day when a man came walking downhill after hitching a ride with a driver from the sawmill.

One morning, as on that earlier occasion, she was outside washing her van when one of the massive vehicles came straining up the grade. But this time, instead of continuing without pause to the plateau a hundred yards above her cabin, the trucker put on the brakes just opposite her driveway.

"Thanks for the lift," a man's voice drifted toward her on the lazy summer air.

Holly crimped the hose and stood stock still. "M-Mack?" she called, swinging her face toward the hazy form ambling across the road.

"I'm looking for a schoolteacher named Smith," responded a familiar voice with a laugh tucked inside it. "How about shutting off the water? I've seen you in action with a hose, and my dress blues wouldn't take kindly to a splashing."

Moaning in frustration, Holly groped her way to the faucet. Couldn't he ever give her a little advance notice? Darn the man! Without her glasses she couldn't even see him properly!

"Why are you wearing your dress blues?" she called

down to him, intrigued by the mental image of elegance.

"Special occasion," Mack replied from the vicinity of the gate. "If you're interested, run inside and get your specs."

Holly fled. "Interested" qualified as the understatement of the year. Reappearing a moment later, her green eyes looked wide with hope and wonder. During her absence, a very smart-looking Marine had walked as far as the porch. He no longer wore his arm in a sling, and no bulging bandages spoiled the fit of the well-tailored jacket. In fact, he looked so fantastic that Holly could only stare at him in mute admiration for a long, heart-stopping moment.

"Special occasion?" she finally managed to croak.

"Yes, ma'am," Mack confirmed. "Very special. First, though, let's get our priorities straight." He shot a glance at the now definitely bedraggled yellow ribbon banding the maple tree. "Yours first. Who did you tie that on there for?"

"You," Holly whispered. "It's hung there through snow and thaw and rain and thunder and lightning, waiting for you to come home."

"I'm back." Mack stepped forward and took her in his arms. "I'm back to stay and I want you with me."

"You want *me*?"

"That's what I tried to tell you last time, only you threw me a curve by insisting we settle important points first. You being a schoolteacher and all, I figured you must be talking about the dull, practical stuff. What I should have said, right up front, was that I love you. But this time, I don't want there to be any mistake about my intentions. Take a look.''

Holly had been feasting her eyes on him, absorbing every flicker of expression, every word. Now, almost reluctantly, she looked away from his face and followed his expansive gesture out to the road.

The logging truck hadn't budged. She gasped as she caught sight of the enormous banner spanning the entire length of the tractor-trailer. A message had been written across it in three-foot-high, red-white-and-blue letters:

I LOVE YOU, HOLLY SMITH! WILL YOU MARRY ME?

''Mack!'' she gasped. ''I thought you only—''

''Wanted a marriage of convenience?'' Mack laughed. ''Honey, it's going to be darned inconvenient if you don't accept this time. Every single person in Spruce Ridge ran out to goggle at that banner when we drove by. You're not going to say no again, are you, sweetheart?''

''Not on your life!'' Holly replied, looking away from the banner that broadcast his feelings for the entire world to see. She lifted her lips for his heartfelt kiss. ''We'll thread yellow ribbons through matching gold rings, and build a partnership to write home about!''

Peering down from the loft window, Jamie whooshed out a sigh of relief as he watched his future parents embrace. He loved Ms. Smith with all his heart. And he loved Mack every bit as much. Never, ever, *ever* could he have chosen between them. And now, nobody would ever ask him to try!